two*way
street

Also from Lauren Barnholdt and Simon Pulse

Watch Me

One Night that Changes Everything

And for younger readers

*The Secret Identity
of Devon Delaney*

two*way street

street

LAUREN BARNHOLDT

SIMON PULSE

New York   London   Toronto   Sydney

SIMON PULSE

An imprint of Simon & Schuster Children's Publishing Division

1230 Avenue of the Americas, New York, NY 10020

Copyright © 2007 by Lauren Barnholdt

All rights reserved, including the right of reproduction

in whole or in part in any form.

SIMON PULSE and colophon are registered trademarks

of Simon & Schuster, Inc.

Designed by Mike Rosamilia

The text of this book was set in Cochin.

Manufactured in the United States of America

First Simon Pulse edition June 2007

14 16 18 20 19 17 15

Library of Congress Control Number 2007920201

ISBN-13: 978-1-4169-1318-4

ISBN-10: 1-4169-1318-1

For my sister, Kelsey, because she begged
and begged to have a book dedicated to her
(and also because she's amazing and wonderful
and makes my book signings a lot more fun)

ACKNOWLEDGMENTS

Thanks to:

My agent, Nadia Cornier, who puts up with my scandalousness on a daily basis and never freaks out about it;

Michelle Nagler, editor extraordinaire, for pushing me to take my books to a whole other level, and for being amazing to work with;

My mom, as always, for being my biggest inspiration;

My sister, Krissi, for always keeping me amused with her text messages;

Robyn Schneider, Kevin Cregg, Kiersten Loerzel, Rob Kean, Abby McDonald, and Scott Neumyer, for being wonderful friends;

My dad, my grandparents, and my whole extended family for all the amazing support;

Aaron Gorvine, for always listening to me, keeping me sane, and constantly telling me not to blog about him;

And, most of all, everyone who read *Reality Chick* and emailed me to tell me they liked it, befriended me on MySpace, or left me a blog comment. You guys rock!

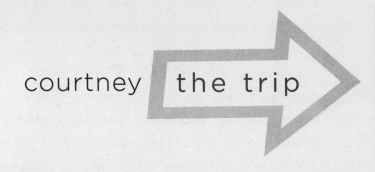

courtney | the trip →

Day One, 8:07 a.m.

I'm a traitor to my generation. Seriously. All we hear about these days is being strong women and standing up for ourselves, and now look what I've done. I should totally be one of those true life stories in *Seventeen*. "I Built My Life Around a Boy! And Now I Regret It!" Of course, it doesn't pack the emotional punch as some of their previous stories, i.e., "I Got An STD Without Having Sex" but it's important nonetheless.

"You're going to be fine," my mom says, stirring her coffee at the sink. "In fact, you're acting a little bit ridiculous."

"I'm ridiculous? I'm ridiculous?" How can she say that? Has she lost her mind? It's so completely *not* ridiculous to be upset about going on a trip with your ex-boyfriend, when said ex-boyfriend broke your heart and left you stranded for some Internet slut. Although I really can't say I know for a fact that she's a slut. But I'm pretty sure she is.

1

I mean, scamming on guys on the Internet? I thought that was only for forty-year-old divorcées who Photoshop their pictures in an effort to appear younger and thinner. Not to mention what was HE thinking? An eighteen-year-old guy who could have any girl he wanted, having to resort to Internet dating? But maybe that's the problem with guys who can have any girl they want. One is never enough.

"I didn't say you *were* ridiculous," my mom says. "I said you're *acting* ridiculous."

"There's really no difference," I tell her. "It's like if someone says 'You're acting like a cheater,' it's because you're cheating. Which means you're a cheater." Like Jordan. Although I suppose technically he isn't a cheater, because he broke up with me before he started dating the Internet girl. In my mind, I still think of him as being a cheater. Otherwise, he just met some girl he liked better, and it's not as dramatic.

"Courtney, you begged and begged to go on this trip," my mom says.

"So?" That's her big justification for calling me ridiculous? Is she kidding? Teenagers beg and beg for stuff all the time—nose rings, tattoos that say "Badass." Never a good idea. My parents are supposed to be the voices of reason, steering me on the right path at all times. They're obviously insane to have agreed to this plan in the first place. I mean, what was I thinking? Making plans to drive over a thousand miles to college with a boy months before we were supposed to go? Everyone knows the average high school relationship is shorter than an episode of *TRL*. "You're the mother," I say. "You should have known this was a horrible idea." I'm hoping to lay a guilt trip on her, but she's not having it.

"Oh, please," she says, rolling her eyes. "How was I supposed to know he was going to break up with you? I'm not psychic. Nor do I know the habits of Internet chat rooms."

"It wasn't a CHAT ROOM," I say. "It was MySpace." No one hangs out in chat rooms anymore. Although why some girl would want to date Jordan based on his MySpace page is beyond me. The song he chose for his profile is "Let's All Get Drunk Tonight" by Afroman.

"Right," my mom says, taking a sip of her coffee. My parents are trying to teach me some kind of lesson. They don't think it's right that they would have to pay more than five hundred dollars for a last-minute plane ticket from Florida to Massachusetts, when I'm the one who convinced them to let me go on this trip. Plus, my mom thinks this whole thing is typical teen angst, one of those situations portrayed on a teen sitcom that's resolved in a half hour of laughs and mishaps. You know, where the girl gets dumped, but then realizes by the end of the show that she's better off without him, and then hooks up with some other hottie who's much better for her, while the guy who broke her heart ends up all alone, wishing he had her back. That is definitely not happening. In fact, it's kind of the other way around. Jordan is having tons of fun with his MySpace girl, while I'm the one sitting around, wishing I had *him* back.

I sigh and stare out the kitchen window, looking for Jordan's TrailBlazer. It's 8:07, and he was supposed to be here at eight, which makes me think that:

a) he's late
b) he's acting like an asshole and blowing me off
or
c) he's gotten into a horrible car crash that's left him dead.

The most likely answer is A. (We went to the prom together, and the limo had to wait in his driveway for half an hour. At the end of the night, we got charged for an extra hour. He—read: his parents—paid for it, but still.) Although I'm all about option C. Okay, maybe not the dead part. Just, like, a broken leg or something. I mean, his parents have always been really nice to me and I would feel horrible if they lost their youngest child. Even if he is a liar and a cheat.

"Do you want some coffee?" my mom asks, which is ridiculous because she knows I don't drink coffee. Coffee stunts your growth. I'm only five-foot-two, and I'm still holding out hope that I'll grow another few inches. Plus I'm tense enough. Getting me all hyped up on caffeine is definitely not a good idea.

"No thanks," I say, looking out the window again. I feel a lump rising in my throat, and I ignore it. He wouldn't blow me off, would he? I mean, that's so screwed up. Although if he did, that means I wouldn't have to go with him. Which would be great. If he stood me up, my parents would have no choice but to let me book a flight and take it to Boston. Which is what they should have let me do in the first place.

I take a deep breath. It's only three days. I can get through that, right? Three days is nothing. Three days is . . . I wrack my brain, trying to think of something that only lasts three days. Christmas vacation! Christmas vacation lasts ten days and it always seems to go by so fast. Three days is only a *third* of that.

Plus, I have the whole thing planned out in minute detail. The trip, I mean. So that every single second, we'll be doing something.

Of course, Christmas vacation is fun. And this is going to be excruciating.

My dad walks into the kitchen, wearing a gray suit and drinking a protein shake. He's humming a Shakira song. My dad loves pop music. Which is weird. Because he's almost fifty. Although I think my dad may be having a bit of a midlife crisis, since lately he's taken to buying weird clothes. And I suspect he's been using self-tanner, because he definitely looks a little orange.

"Good morning," he says, heading over to where my mom is sitting at the kitchen table and planting a kiss on her head. He opens the cupboard and pulls down a box of cereal.

"Morning," I mumble, not sure what's so good about it.

"All set for school?" he asks, smiling.

"Yeah, I guess," I say, trying not to sound like too much of a brat. My dad has been way cooler about this whole breakup thing than my mom. He's spent hours trying to cheer me up by telling me I'd meet someone better, there's more fish in the sea, he never liked Jordan, etc. Plus he bought me a new iPod and tons of new clothes for school. He also slipped me a copy of *He's Just Not That Into You*, which I guess he thought was empowering. It actually kind of *is* empowering, because it talks about how you shouldn't settle for a guy who doesn't want to be with you. On the other hand, realizing the guy you like "just isn't that into you" is not very good for one's self-esteem. Plus I was reading parts of it to my friend Jocelyn one time, and she interrupted me to say, "Actually, if you need a book like that to tell you he's just not that into you, you're probably not the type that's going to actually be able to let go." She wasn't trying to say it about me, exactly, but still.

"Jordan here yet?" my dad asks, pouring milk over his cereal.

"Of course not," I say. "Hey, if he doesn't show up, then what?"

"You think he won't show up?" my dad asks, glancing up. "Why wouldn't he?"

"I don't know." I say. "But what if he doesn't?" Hope starts to rise up inside me. There's no way either one of my parents can or want to drive me. I won't even feel bad about the money they'll have to spend on a last-minute plane ticket, since they're the psychos who are making me go on this trip in the first place. "Then what?" I persist.

But no one has to answer that, because the sound of gravel crunching on the driveway outside comes through the window. I look out, and the light shines off the windshield of Jordan's TrailBlazer and hits my eyes.

Some kind of ridiculous rap music is blasting from the car, which makes me even more annoyed than I already am. I hate rap music. He doesn't even listen to normal rap, like Jay-Z or Nelly. He listens to "hardcore" rap. (His word, not mine. I've never used the word "hardcore" in my life. Well, until right now, and then only to quote Jordan.)

I ignore the weird feeling in my stomach and run outside so I can yell at him for being late. "Where have you been?" I demand as he gets out of the car.

"Nice to see you, too." He smiles. He's wearing baggie tan shorts and a navy blue Abercrombie T-shirt. His dark hair is wet, which means he probably just got out of the shower, which means he probably just woke up. "I'm sorry, I was packing my stuff, and then I was trying to find my parents so I could say good-bye to them."

Packing his stuff? Who waits until the day they're leaving

for college to start packing their stuff? My stuff's been packed for a week, neatly stacked outside my bedroom door until I moved it into the kitchen this morning. I mean, the housing office sent us a packing list. Of stuff to bring. I'll bet Jordan doesn't have any of it. Not like I care. If he wants to sleep on an empty, disgusting, stained mattress because he forgot to purchase extra-long sheets, that's fine with me. I'm so over him. This is me, being over him. La, la, la.

"Didn't you get my email?" I ask him. Three days ago I emailed him a copy of our trip itinerary. It was really short, with a subject line that simply said "Schedule" and read, "Jordan, Attached, please find a copy of the schedule for our trip. Best, Courtney." I was really proud of it. The email, I mean. Because it was so short and cold. Of course, it took me and my friend Jocelyn about two hours to come up with the perfect wording, but Jordan doesn't know that. He just must think I'm too important to compose long email messages with him, or get ensconsed in a back-and-forth email exchange. Not that he ever emailed me back. But it was obviously because I was so cold.

"The one about the trip?" He frowns. "Yeah, I think so."

"You think so?" I ask.

"Court, you can't plan everything to the minute," he says. "There are going to be setbacks." He takes the sunglasses that are on his head and slides them down over his eyes.

"Well, whatever," I say. Luckily I have three copies of the trip itinerary, along with specific MapQuest instructions all printed out and paper-clipped together. I'll give him one to reference. I start to walk into the house, and Jordan hesitates.

"Are you going to help me with my stuff or not?" I ask.

"Oh, yeah, sure." I raise my eyebrows. "Of course," he repeats more forcefully.

He follows me into the house, and I can tell he's staring at my ass. Pervert.

"Jordan," my dad says, nodding. Jordan nods back but doesn't say anything. I hope he's scared of my dad. If he isn't, he should be. My dad's kind of a big guy. Not that Jordan's scrawny or anything. In fact, just the opposite. He has these really amazing arms that—Ugh. I will not think about any part of Jordan's lying, cheating, never-on-time body, arms or otherwise.

"Excited to be going to school?" my mom asks politely. Her tone is guarded, which makes me happy. When Jordan and I were together, she was always supernice to him. She might be making me go on this trip, but it's obvious where her loyalties lie. I hope Jordan is uncomfortable. I hope he's squirming. I hope he's—

"Yes, ma'am," he says. Which is total bullshit. He could care less, obviously. I mean, he didn't even follow the packing list.

"Whatever," I say, putting my hands on my temples like I can't take it anymore. "Can you start loading up the car? I don't want to be any later than we already are." I give Jordan a pointed look, which he ignores, and then point him in the direction of my stuff, which is packed neatly and piled on the kitchen floor.

"Jesus, Court," he says, looking at the mound. "You know you're only going for four years, right?" I ignore him and pull a copy of the schedule out of my pocket.

"We are way behind," I say, frowning. We were supposed to have left twenty minutes ago. Although maybe if we don't stop for lunch and just drive straight through, we can make up the time that way. Still, it's not good to be starting off late. I've budgeted for traffic and unforeseen circumstances of course, but still. This should not count as an unforeseen circumstance. An unforeseen circumstance is something that you can't avoid. And this could definitely have been avoided.

Jordan reaches down and picks up one of the bags that's on the ground near my feet, and it brushes against my toe.

"Ow!" I say, jumping back. "Watch it. I'm wearing sandals."

He smiles. "Sorry, honey." He turns and heads out to the car before I can reply. I take a deep breath. I will not start fighting with him. There's no way. If I start fighting with him, he's going to know that he's getting to me, and I can't let that happen. The last thing I need is for him to think I'm upset about him breaking up with me. I've spent the past two weeks determined to show him I don't care, and I'm not going to screw it all up now. Of course, it's much easier to pretend you don't care about someone when they're not around you, but I can do it. I just have to gather all my self-control. Disengage and detach is my new motto.

I realize my heart is beating at a ridiculously abnormal rate, and I take another deep breath. I can do this, I tell myself. I start thinking of all the hot guys I'm going to meet in college. Guys who read philosophy books and drink coffee. Guys who listen to real music, like Mozart and Andrea Bocelli and maybe even Gavin DeGraw. Anything but rap music. It makes me feel better, but only for a second. Because, let's face it—no matter how much you tell yourself you're over someone, your heart knows the truth.

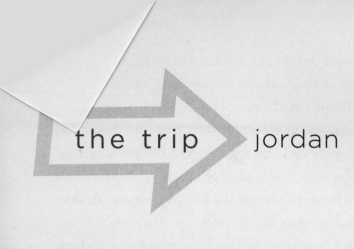

the trip > jordan

Day One, 8:37 a.m.

I can't figure out why Courtney is wearing such tight clothing. Do girls normally wear short pink cotton skirts and tight tank tops while going on a road trip? I've seen that ridiculous Britney Spears movie *Crossroads*, and I definitely don't remember the girls in that movie wearing such slutty clothes. T-shirts and track pants is what they wore. Is she doing it in an effort to drive me insane? And is she going to act like a bitch the whole time? It's not my fault I was late. I had to pack my stuff, which you would think would be easy—just throw your clothes, computer, and CDs into a suitcase, right? Wrong. It took fucking forever. But I was trying to hurry—I didn't even gel my hair, which was a pretty big sacrifice. When it finally dries I'm going to look like Seth Cohen or some shit.

My cell phone rings as I'm loading Courtney's stuff into the back of my truck and trying not to think about the next three days.

I answer it without checking the caller ID.

"Yeah," I say, lifting a pink bag with long straps into the back. What the hell does she have in here? It feels like weights.

"Yo," my best friend, B. J. Cartwright, says, sounding wide awake, which is surprising. B. J. never sounds wide awake. Especially since he's usually either hungover, drunk, or getting ready to get drunk.

"Yo," I say, sitting down on my open truck bed. "What's up?"

"Breaking news, dude," he says, sounding nervous. B. J. always has breaking news. It used to always involve some girl he wanted to bang, but for the past few months, he's been going out with Courtney's friend Jocelyn. He's still the biggest gossip I know, and one of his deepest secrets is that he subscribes to *Us Weekly*.

"Is that why you're up so early?"

"Huh? Oh, no, I haven't been to sleep yet," he says.

"You've been up all night?" I ask, glancing at my watch. "It's nine o'clock in the morning."

"Dude, the party went until four this morning," he says. "And then we all went to breakfast. You missed a great fucking time."

Last night's party was kind of a last hurrah, a sendoff before everyone left for school, which most people are doing this weekend. I was there for a while, but I took off before things got really crazy. I knew I had to be up early this morning so I wouldn't piss Courtney off by being late. Look how well that turned out.

"So what's the breaking news?" I ask.

"It's about Courtney," he says, and I feel my stomach drop.

"What about her?" I say.

"She's hooking up with Lloyd," he says, and I swallow hard. Figures. Lloyd is Courtney's best friend, this total tool who Court's been in love with since like seventh grade. Well, until she met me. Supposedly as soon as we started dating, she lost all her feelings for him. Or so she said.

"How do you know?" I ask, not sure I want to hear about this.

"Heard it from Julianna Fields, who heard it from Lloyd."

"When?"

"Not sure," B. J. says. "She was talking about it last night. After the party, really late. And then, um, Lloyd left Courtney a MySpace comment last night."

"Well, whatever," I say. I stand up, load the rest of the bags into the back of my truck, and slam it shut. "Courtney can do whatever the hell she wants."

"You okay?"

"I'm fine," I lie. "Thanks for letting me know."

"Cool," B. J. says. "Call me later."

I click off my cell phone and take a deep breath. Whatever. This isn't a big deal. I mean, *I* broke up with *her*. All I have to do is get through the next three days. Three days is nothing. Three days is half of spring break. Spring break flew by in two seconds this year. Thinking about spring break makes me start thinking about vacations, which makes me start thinking about Courtney and me in Miami, and the bathing suit she was wearing, and what happened on the beach. . . . Stop. I tell myself. It's over.

I take another deep breath, and when I turn around Courtney's dad is standing there, holding his briefcase in one hand and a cup of coffee in the other.

"All packed up?" he says, smiling. I do my best to smile back, and resist the urge to punch him.

"Looks like it," I say. I feel my fists clench at my side, and I will myself to unclench them.

"We're clear on everything, right, Jordan?" he says. He leans in close to me, and I can smell his aftershave. "I would hate for this trip to end in a bad way, with Courtney getting distracted before her first day of school."

"I wouldn't want Courtney to get upset either," I say, which is true. What I don't add is that if her father wasn't such an asshole, there'd be no chance of Courtney finding out anything that would upset her in the first place.

"Great," he says, clapping me on the shoulder like we're old friends. "I'm glad we're on the same page." He studies me for a minute, but I don't break my gaze. "I *am* going to tell her, you know."

"Of course," I say, even though he's been feeding me the same bullshit line for the past three months.

15

He hesitates for a minute, like he wants to say something else, or is waiting for me to reassure him that I'm not going to talk. But I'm not going to. Reassure him. Or talk. But he doesn't need to know that.

"Have a safe trip," he says finally, and then takes off down the driveway.

Once he's out of sight, I lean my head against the side of my truck and take a deep breath. I've spent the past two weeks driving myself completely crazy with the fact that if it weren't for Courtney's douchebag dad, and one second that changed everything, we'd still be together. But instead, we're not, and Courtney hates me.

And who could blame her? She thinks I dumped her for some girl I met on the Internet. If she knew what really happened, she'd probably hate me even more. Because the truth is, Courtney and I broke up for a really fucked-up reason that she doesn't know about, and hopefully never will. There is no Internet girl. I made her up.

jordan 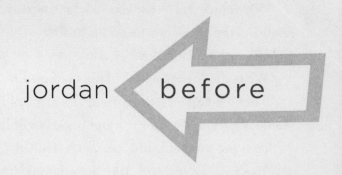 before

125 Days Before the Trip, 9:02 p.m.

I pull my TrailBlazer into my friend B. J.'s driveway and lay on the horn. B. J.'s real name is Brian Joseph Cartwright, but in seventh grade everyone started calling him B. J. We'd all just found out about the term "blow job," and we thought the nickname was super witty and cool. After a few years, it got old to everyone except B. J. He still loves the name and refuses to answer to anything else, even from teachers.

B. J. comes out of the house wearing a green bodysuit, green booties, and a leprechaun hat. I'm less concerned with what he's wearing, and more concerned about the fact that he's moving about as fast as a dial-up connection. We're on our way to Connor Mitchell's party, and I don't want to miss a second of it.

He opens the door (slowly) and launches himself into the passenger seat of my truck.

"Whaddup, kid?" he asks. He slams the door shut and readjusts the green beanie on his head.

"What the fuck is this?" I ask.

"What the fuck is what?" He's confused.

"This whole leprechaun thing," I say, rolling my eyes. I readjust my sideview mirror and back out of his driveway.

"I am not a leprechaun!" he says, offended. "I'm a midget."

"You're a midget?" I ask, incredulous. "You're dressed like a leprechaun. And they don't call them midgets anymore, they call them 'little people.'" I pull my eyes away from the road and glance at him quickly. Is it possible he's drunk already?

"I'm a little person, then," he says, sounding like he doesn't give a shit. "But really, who cares? I'm going to be so wasted it isn't going to matter."

"The only reason it's kind of weird," I say slowly, not wanting to upset him, "is because it's not a costume party. So I don't understand why you'd be dressed up."

"It's not a costume party?" he asks, sounding confused again. "I thought Madison said something about going as a cheerleader." He rolls down his window, which makes no sense, because the air conditioner is on. I don't understand why people have to roll down their windows when the air conditioner is on, since it's obviously hotter outside than it is in the car.

"No," I say, "Madison *is* a cheerleader. Why would she go to a costume party dressed as one?"

"She said she was going to!"

"She said she might not have time to change after the game, and might need to wear her uniform to the party." Madison Allesio is this blonde sophomore who's in study hall with B. J. and me. She's also the reason I'm going to this party tonight. Well, kind of. I probably would have gone anyway, since Connor Mitchell is known to throw some insane parties. Last year half the freshman class was topless in his pool. But Madison's been flirting with me hardcore for the past month, and yesterday she was all, "Are you going to Connor's party?" But she said it in a "Are you going to Connor's party so I can go home with you and get it on?" kind of way.

"I don't give a shit," B. J. says, grinning. "I'm going to be so fucked up I won't even care. And I'm a leprechaun, and you know leprechauns are always gettin' lucky! Woot woot!" He pumps his hands in the air in a "raise the roof" gesture. B. J. is always talking about how much play he's going to get, when in reality, he gets none.

We hear the party before we get there, a mix of what sounds like mainstream rap. Jay-Z, 50 Cent, that kind of stuff. Posers. I like my rap hard and dirty, none of this "top forty" bullshit. But once I get a few beers in me, and a few girls on me, I'm sure I'll be fine. I maneuver my car into a parking spot on the street and follow B. J. up the walk and into the house.

Half an hour later, I'm starting to think this party might

actually blow. B. J. was entertaining me for a while, but now he's disappeared into the throng of people somewhere after doing a keg stand, and I have no idea where he is.

I'm sitting in Connor's living room, deciding whether or not to get up and get another beer, when I feel a pair of hands across my eyes.

"Hey," a female voice says behind me. "Guess who?" She's leaning over me now, and I catch a whiff of perfume. I can tell it's Madison from how she smells — good, and like you'd want to get her naked immediately.

"I don't know," I say, playing dumb. "Jessica?" I don't even know any Jessicas. I'm such a stud.

"No," she says, trying to sound hurt.

"Jennifer? Jamie?"

"Not a *J* name," she says. She's closer now, and I can feel her chest pushing into the back of my head.

"I give up," I say, reaching up to pull her hands off my eyes.

Madison pouts her lips and puts a hand on her hips. "It's Madison!" she says, puffing out her lip. She's wearing a short white skirt and a pink halter top. I was kind of hoping she'd be in her cheerleader uniform, but she looks hot anyway. Her long blond hair falls in waves down her back. It's all I can do not to pick her up and take her back to my truck with me.

"Ahhh, Madison," I say. "I was looking for you."

"You were not," she says, sighing. "You didn't even know it was me."

This is what confuses me about girls like Madison. They're hot, they could have any guy they want, and yet they spend most of their time trying to get guys to *tell* them they're hot. It doesn't make sense. It's like they don't want to believe they're good-looking. Or maybe they just get off on having guys tells them over and over.

(Another note about girls like Madison: They're good for hookups, but are not girlfriend material. Inevitably, you get tired of listening to them whine about whether or not you think they're hot, and they have to go. Plus, if you date a girl like Madison, you run the risk of actually starting to like her, and then she will eventually end up dumping you for some new guy who tells her how beautiful she is, because she's sick of hearing it from you. The trick is to play into their egos enough to keep them around, but not so much that they become bored. Luckily, I am a master at this.)

"I was looking for you," I repeat. I try to look disinterested and take a sip of my drink. "You look hot." I scan the crowd behind her, still not looking at her.

"Really?" she asks, looking pleased. She does a little twirl, and her skirt fans out around her legs. Which are really, really tan. And really, really long. I try not to stare, knowing that if I let myself get too worked up, I won't be able to continue playing the game. Hormones are such a bitch.

"So you never responded to my MySpace message," I say, and her face flushes. My last MySpace message was about how hot her lips looked, and how I couldn't wait to kiss her.

"I never got it," she says, but I can tell she's lying. She looks over to where her friends are standing on the other side of the room. "This party is so lame." She glances at me out of the corner of her eye, and I know that's my signal.

"You want to get out of here?" I ask. "I have my truck."

She shrugs, like she doesn't care. "I guess. Just let me go tell my friends."

Madison walks away, and I try to find some way to distract myself. I can't be waiting for her when she comes back. I have to make her work for it a little. I know it sounds mean and fucked up, but it really isn't. It's just how things work. I look around for some situation that has to be taken care of, or some girl I know that I can later claim came up to me, not vice versa. And that's when I see B. J. attached to Courtney McSweeney's leg.

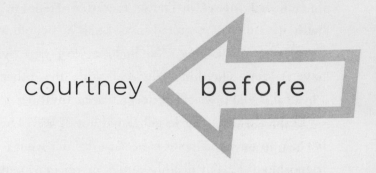

courtney before

125 Days Before the Trip, 9:43 p.m.

Tonight I'm going to tell my friend Lloyd that I'm in love with him. Important things about Lloyd:

1. He's been my best friend since the seventh grade, when we got seated near each other in every single class because of our last names. It seemed like every teacher was doing it alphabetically, so since I'm McSweeney and he's McPeak, we were always together. When we got to high school and ended up being able to choose our own seats, we still sat together. It was like a rule.

2. Ever since the first day of seventh grade, I've been in love with him. My friend Jocelyn says that you can't be in love with someone if:

   a) they don't know it
   b) they don't feel the same way
   c) you've never kissed them, held hands with them, or done anything more than be friends with them.

But that makes no sense to me whatsoever, because, hello, it's called unrequited love. Look at people in movies. They're always saying "I'm in love with you" when they haven't done anything physical with the other person. Physical is just physical, it doesn't *mean* anything.

Besides, I *am* going to tell Lloyd how I feel. The reason I haven't up until this point is because I don't want to ruin the friendship (i.e., I'm deathly afraid of rejection). But lately, there have been signs. Lloyd has been calling me every single night—definitely more than usual—and talking on the phone with me for hours. And he helps me with my math homework, even when I get totally confused and it takes us twenty minutes to do one problem. He never gets impatient with me.

I have to make my move soon, though, because Lloyd is going to school in North Carolina and I'm going to school in Boston, so we're going to need to be dating for a few months before we leave for college. That way we'll be all set up for a long-distance relationship. Which is why I plan on telling him. Tonight. After the party. That I want to be more than friends.

I'm even wearing my "I'm going to tell Lloyd I want him" outfit, which consists of a very short jean skirt and a tight white shirt. Which is not the kind of thing I usually wear. But I need to get Lloyd to stop thinking of me as a friend and start thinking of me as someone he wants to date.

So far, the night is not going as planned. First, Lloyd said he would be at this party, and so far, I have not seen him. Second, my friend Jocelyn (who I drove here with), is off talking to this junior guy she has a crush on and has left me standing here by myself. This is not her fault, because I told her I would be fine, since I thought Lloyd would be here soon, and I would be so busy seducing him that I wouldn't need Jocelyn to hang out with me anyway. Third, and definitely the most upsetting, is that right at this moment, there is a guy dressed like a leprechaun with his arms wrapped around my legs. I'm scandalized by this, but I'm trying to be nice, because I think he's drunk.

"Oh, um, hi," I say, trying to push him away gently. "You're, um, a leprechaun." This is why I don't go to parties. Because stuff like this always happens to me. I'm always the one standing in some corner, by myself, with a guy dressed like a leprechaun drooling on my leg.

"I am not," he says, looking up at me. "I'm a midget." I get a good look at his face and realize it's B. J. Cartwright. Great. The craziest guy in the senior class is wrapped around my leg. B. J.'s done some pretty insane stuff, including burning our class name and year into the lawn outside the front doors of our school. He almost got expelled for it, but the school board relented since no one got hurt. B. J. put condoms in all the teachers' mailboxes on Safe Sex Awareness Day, rigged the school penny contest so that our class would win, and showed up on Halloween as Hannah Baker, a girl in our class who got arrested over the summer for prostitution. He wore balloon boobs and everything.

"A midget," I say, trying to disentangle myself from him again, but he has a viselike grip on my leg. "That's, erhm, interesting."

"You've always wanted to do it with a midget, haven't you, Britney?" he asks, licking his lips at me. Oh, my God.

"My name's not Britney," I say, hoping maybe he's looking for someone specific, and once he realizes I'm not her, he'll take off.

"I know it's not," he says, rolling his eyes. "But you look like her."

"Like Britney?" I ask, confused. His hands feel sticky against my bare leg, and I curse myself for wearing a skirt.

"Yes," he slurs, leering at me. "You look like Britney Spears."

"Really?" I ask, pleased in spite of myself. Then it occurs to me that Britney's gone through several stages of attractiveness, and I wonder if he means I look like Hot Britney, or Not So Hot Britney, I consider asking him to clarify but I'm not sure I could handle the answer.

Still, no one has told me I look like a celebrity before. In fact, one time Jocelyn tried to set me up with this guy online, and the first thing he asked me was who my celebrity lookalike was. And I told him "No one, I look like myself," which, you know, was definitely kind of lame. Because even if I DON'T have a celebrity lookalike, I could have made something up, or just given a vague idea, like, "Well, I have long dark hair like Rachel Bilson," or something. Not that it would have worked out anyway. The relationship with the online guy, I mean. He told me his celebrity lookalike was Jake Gyllenhaal, and I hadn't even asked him for the information. He just volunteered it. Which meant that he was dying for me to know, which meant that he was totally conceited. I can't deal with conceited. (Actually, I probably could deal with a little conceit, but I think I was just scared because there's no way I'd feel comfortable going out with a guy who looks like Jake Gyllenhaal. That would not be good for my self-esteem.)

"Yes," B. J. says. "You look just like Britney." He reaches up and pokes me in the stomach. "Except for her abs. You don't have her abs." His face falls. All right then.

"Um, Britney's had kids," I say. "And so her abs, I'm sure, are shot." He considers this, nods, and then licks my leg. Gross.

"Okay, you need to knock that off." I stick my leg out and try to shake him off, but it's harder than it looks. Even though he's dressed like a midget, and has been walking around on his knees all night, B. J. is six-foot-four and probably weighs close to two hundred pounds. He's *heavy*. I look around for Jocelyn, but I can't find her anywhere. Typical. She begs me to come to this party, and then leaves me right at the crucial moment, i.e., when I have a midget-leprechaun attached to my leg. "Stop!" I command, wondering if I can stick the heel of my shoe into his stomach without really hurting him.

"Why?" he asks. "I'm helping you with your midget fetish." He licks my leg again. Oh, *eww*.

"I do NOT have a midget fetish!" I say, louder this time, hoping that my change of volume will help him get the message.

"Not yet." He grins up at me, and I'm about to stick my heel right into his stomach, not caring if it causes permanent damage or not, when Jordan Richman appears out of the crowd and picks B. J. up by his elbows.

"All right, Lucky," he says, removing B. J. from my leg, swinging him around, and placing him a safe few feet away. Oh, thank God. Jordan must be really strong to be able to pick up B. J. like that. Although, once he set him down, B. J. went limp and fell to the ground, so maybe he was so drunk that it didn't matter how big he was Kind of like when you're in water, your weight doesn't matter. Maybe it's the same when you're drunk. "I think that's enough."

"Whaddup, kid?" B. J. asks Jordan. He grins at him and readjusts the green beanie on his head.

"Nothing," Jordan says, looking slightly amused, "but you can't just go around humping people's legs." He rolls his eyes.

"I wasn't humping her!" B. J. says, offended. "I'm a midget."

"You're not a midget," I say, before I can stop myself. "You're dressed like a leprechaun. And they don't call them midgets anymore, they call them 'little people.'" Jordan grins at me.

"I'm a little person, then," he says, sounding cheerful. "But, really, who cares? I'm so wasted it doesn't matter."

"It's not a costume party," I point out.

"I know," B. J. says sadly. "But Madison said she might wear her cheerleading uniform."

"But she didn't," Jordan says.

I don't understand what Madison's cheerleading uniform has to do with it being a costume party, but I know enough to realize they're talking about Madison Allesio. It figures Jordan would be friends with her. There's this rumor going around that she likes to do this oral sex thing with Kool-Aid. Something to do with, uh, different flavors for different guys. Totally disgusting, which seems kind of like Jordan's type. Not that I know him all that well. We're in the same math class, and that's about it. But one time I heard him in the hall before class, arguing with a girl. Something about how she needed to stop following him around. And then she said he shouldn't have hooked up with her if he didn't want a girlfriend. It was actually kind of a math class scandal, because the whole class could hear everything that was going on. Finally, I think he just walked into the classroom while she was screaming. I couldn't see the girl, but later on I found out it was this freshman named Katie Shaw, and then I really didn't feel so bad about the whole thing, because I know for a fact she messes around with a lot of guys—including Lloyd, who she went to third base with in a movie theater. Anyway, the point is, I'm not surprised

Jordan's friends with Madison. He apparently likes girls who thrive on hookups and drama.

"I don't give a shit." B. J. shrugs. "I'm a leprechaun. And leprechauns. Get. Lucky." He pumps his hands in the air in a "raise the roof" gesture. "Besides," he continues, grinning, "Britney liked it." He grins at me again and then waddles off on his knees.

"Sorry about that," Jordan says, smiling sheepishly. "He gets crazy when he's drunk. But he wouldn't have done anything."

"It's okay," I say, feeling stupid.

"Here," he says, pulling a tissue out of his pocket and handing it to me.

"Thanks." I wipe B. J.'s saliva off my leg and check my skin to make sure it's not broken, all the while scanning my brain for diseases that can be transferred by bites. I can't think of any. Lyme disease, maybe? But I don't think you can get that from other people, just from ticks. They should totally concentrate on communicable bite diseases in health class, since apparently I have more of a chance of getting bitten than I do of losing my virginity.

"Anyway, it's Courtney, right?"

"Yeah," I say, surprised that he's asking. He should know my name. We've been in the same advanced math class for four years.

He smiles at me, his eyes shining. "Sorry, that was lame. I know your name. I was just trying to be smooth."

I laugh and so does he.

"Are you here by yourself?" he asks, looking around.

"No," I say quickly, so he doesn't think I'm a total loser. "My friend Jocelyn is here somewhere, but I lost track of her."

"Yeah," he says. "I try to keep an eye on B. J. when he starts drinking, but it's hard with this many people here."

"I can imagine," I say, trying to think of something cool to say. Not that I'm interested in him or anything. I mean, he's cute enough, but that's not why I can't think of anything cool to say. I just have a hard time with small talk. My friend Jocelyn says I'm too quiet. But I'm really not quiet. I just tend to come across that way to new people because I don't like to talk first. What if the other person doesn't want to be bothered? I wonder if I should ask Jordan if he knows what kind of diseases can be transmitted through saliva.

"Anyway, you wanna dance?" he asks, gesturing to one side of the party, where everyone is dancing to a top forty remix.

"Oh, no thanks," I say, trying not to look horrified. There's no way I'm dancing at this party. If he'd ever seen me dance, he would know why. I am not a good dancer. I *like* to dance, I'm just not very good at it. I like to keep my dancing confined to my room, where I can pretend to be Christina or Rhianna without anyone watching.

"Oh," he says, looking confused. Probably no girls have

ever turned him down to dance before. He looks at me, and I realize he's waiting for an explanation, some kind of reason why I can't dance.

"I would," I say quickly, hoping he doesn't think I'm a dork and/or leave. It's not that I'm loving talking to him or anything, but I don't want to be the only loser at the party talking to no one. That's how I got accosted by a leprechaun. "But my leg kind of hurts." This is a total lie. Besides the fact that every time I think of what just happened, my leg feels kind of slimy, I actually feel fine. I mean, B. J. didn't bite me or anything. He just sort of slobbered on me. Which was, you know, unpleasant and everything, but didn't hurt.

"Oh, I'm sorry," Jordan says, looking genuinely concerned. Which makes me feel bad. But I would much rather deal with the guilt of lying about a medical condition than the humiliation of having to dance in front of everyone here. "Do you think you need to go to the doctor or anything?"

"Oh, no, I don't think it's that bad," I say, "but I probably shouldn't, uh, dance on it or anything."

"Okay," he agrees. He keeps looking over his shoulder for something (someone? B. J.?), which is kind of distracting.

There's a pause, and I take a sip of my soda in an effort to appear busy. I finally spot Jocelyn across the room, where she's sitting on an oversized leather couch, talking to a different guy than the one she originally left me for. She gives me a look and raises her eyebrows, like, "What's the deal?" I try to telegraph back, "Absolutely nothing!" But she gives me a "Yeah, right" look back. I know she's thinking about Lloyd.

"Hey," Jordan says, looking around again. What is he looking for? Maybe he lost something. Or maybe someone stole something from him, and now he's looking for whoever took it. Or maybe he wants to make sure his midget friend is okay. "How does your leg feel now?"

"Fine, thanks," I say without thinking. "Much better."

"Great," he says. "Miraculous recovery." He takes the drink I'm holding out of my hand and sets it down on the table next to us. "Then you can dance."

"Oh, no," I say, panicked. "I don't think I'm ready for that." Putting on a Destiny's Child iTunes mix and rocking out in your room while pretending to be Beyoncé is one thing. Actually dancing in front of people from school is another thing. Plus, what if I get all sweaty or fall or something? And then later, Lloyd is like, "You know what, Courtney? I would have gone out with you, except since tonight I saw you looking like a sweaty, clumsy mess. I'm going to have to pass." I don't think I'm ready to risk my chance of happiness with Lloyd over one dance.

"Come on," Jordan says, taking my hand. "You'll be fine." He looks at me and smiles, and I hesitate.

"I don't dance," I admit, going for the truth.

"I'll be gentle," he promises, and before I can protest, he's dragging me out onto the dance floor.

the trip > courtney

Day One, 9:12 a.m.

"So," I say, putting on my seat belt and settling in to the car. "Now that we're completely late and are going to miss orientation . . ." I trail off, hoping he realizes the error of his ways. The error of his ways being, you know, that we'll miss orientation and end up failing out of college because of it. Who knows what could happen if we don't get oriented? It could be bad. We could end up lost and out of it for four years, wrecking our future because we missed some vital information that was given out exclusively during orientation.

"We're not going to miss orientation," he says, pulling down the rearview mirror and checking his reflection.

"Hello? Could you spend less time grooming yourself and more time, like, actually driving?" His hair is a mess. Rumpled, like he just got out of bed. It's actually kind of cute. But I'm not going to miss college just because he didn't have time to do his hair. Or because he's cute. I've lost enough of my self-respect.

"Like, okay," he says, doing a pretty good impression of my voice. He smiles and pulls the sunglasses on his head back down over his eyes. He starts the car. It sputters and stops, and I look at him in alarm.

"Just kidding," he says. He winks and starts the car. Ugh. What an ass. How can he joke at a time like this? I mean, even if he's not concerned about the fact that we're going to miss our orientation, he should still be upset that we're going on this trip and are broken up.

There's silence for a few minutes as he pulls out of my driveway. I reach into my bag and pull out my book, determined to ignore him. I'm reading *The Catcher in the Rye* for the millionth time, figuring it's

a) funny

b) about a kid who goes crazy, so I won't feel so bad about myself, and

c) I won't have to worry about comprehending it, since I've already read it a million times.

I reach down and push my seat back.

"Whatcha readin'?" Jordan asks politely.

"Like you care." I snort. I don't think I've ever seen Jordan pick up a book in his life. I reach over and turn down the car CD player, which is playing some kind of ridiculous rap music. "I can't concentrate on my book."

He shrugs.

"Hey," I say, realizing he's not headed the right way. "You're not going the right way."

"Oh," he says. "Yeah, I know. I thought we could grab some breakfast." He says this like he doesn't know it will upset me, which upsets me even more than if he had been apologetic.

"But I have a schedule," I say, trying not to start a fight this early in the game. The last thing I want is to set him off. "And we're already behind."

"But I'm hungry."

"Well, you should have eaten before you left," I say. If he wasn't eating breakfast, then what was he doing?

"I told you," he says, "I was packing my stuff."

"Well, whatever," I say. "You should have planned properly."

"Look, we can stop really quick at Johni's Diner," he says. "We can pick up the highway right there, and it won't be that much out of our way."

"Yes, but we're already behind schedule," I say, waving the itinerary in front of his face. "So we should actually be trying to make up time, not get further behind."

"Look, if we don't stop now, we're just going to have to—" The sound of his cell phone rings, cutting him off. He has it programmed to play Sir Mix-a-Lot's "Baby Got Back," which is so corny, because that song is so 1999. And he doesn't even like big butts. I don't think. Unless I have a huge ass and don't know it.

He checks the caller ID briefly and then slides the phone open. He has one of those phones that's also a mini computer and plays MP3s. Of course. His parents buy him everything.

"Hey," he says into the headpiece, glancing at me out of the corner of his eye. He catches me looking at him, and I turn away, reaching into the backseat. I rummage around in one of my bags for the CD I burned last night.

"No, we're on our way," Jordan says, sounding strained. It's probably his MySpace girl. I don't exactly know her name, or anything about her, but that's not from lack of trying. I searched his MySpace profile obsessively but I couldn't find anything. You'd think she would have left him a comment or something, right? But then I thought maybe he figured I would have searched, so he told her not to. Or deleted them. And then, just when I was starting to really obsess, he switched the age of his profile to "14" so that no one could look at it. MySpace has this rule where if you're fourteen or younger, your profile automatically gets set to private, and only the people you have friended can view it. So Jordan switched his age and then took me off his friends list! Which was really a horrible thing to do when you think about it, because it was, like, an actual act of aggression. I mean, it's one thing to dump me for another girl, but to actually block me on MySpace? That's just rude. He blocked me on instant messenger, too. And I couldn't even go through and make up a fake screen name, because he had everyone who wasn't on his buddy list blocked.

But I know she's from Tampa (the new girl, I mean), and that she's going to Boston College. Which is supposedly how she found him. She was searching MySpace profiles for people who were going to college in Boston. I'm surprised he didn't offer her a ride.

How I imagine Jordan's new girlfriend (A Psychotic Delusion by Courtney Elizabeth McSweeney):

1. She's blonde. I have dark hair and fair skin. (Even though I live in Florida, I tend to burn when I sit out in the sun, which sucks, because everyone at school is always tan. At least in Boston, I won't have to worry about that.) She also has blue eyes and dark skin. She looks like one of those girls on *Laguna Beach*. I have no idea why I think this, because one time we were watching *Laguna Beach* together, and Jordan told me he thought all the girls on that show looked alike. I guess it's because I figure he would leave me for someone who was completely my opposite, and that includes physically.

2. She has a tattoo of a butterfly or some sort of pink design on her lower back. She wears lots of low-rise jeans.

3. She likes pop music, and she loves to go dancing. In my deluded fantasies, her and Jordan are always going clubbing. She's also one of the worst kind of girls, the kind that all the guys want and drool all over, but

is completely trustworthy and never does anything behind her boyfriend's back.

4. She's rich.

5. She's not a virgin, and her and Jordan do it all over the place. In fact, she wants to do it so much that Jordan can't even keep up with her. He's tired all the time. She's always tearing off her clothes and throwing herself at him.

I find the CD in my bag and rustle around some more, trying to make it out like I'm looking for something else. The last thing I want is for him to think I'm listening to his conversation with Mercedes (that's what I imagine her name to be), even though that's totally what I'm doing.

"Okay, cool," he says. He snaps the phone shut and drops it onto the console between our seats. I rustle around some more, wondering what a good amount of time is to come back up without being obvious. At least he didn't say "I love you" when they hung up. Although maybe they usually do, but he didn't want to say it in front of me, since he was afraid I'd go psychotic on him or something. Which I wouldn't have done. Gone psychotic, I mean. At least not out loud.

"What are you looking for?" he asks. Although it may be a little too early for them to be saying "I love you" to each other, right? I mean, they've only been together two weeks. The thought of Jordan saying "I love you" to another girl makes me feel like I want to throw up. I sit back up quickly, holding the CD.

"This," I tell him.

Then *my* phone starts ringing, and I ignore it, because:

a) I think it's rude to talk on cell phones when you're in the car with someone, and since I want to reserve the right to give Jordan shit about it in the future, I don't think I should be hypocritical now.

b) It's probably Jocelyn, calling to ask me if I'm okay, and she's going to ask a million questions, and I won't be able to really talk to her, because I'll only be able to give one-word answers, like "yes" and "no" and Jordan will obviously know that we're talking about him, otherwise why would I be giving one-word answers?

"I Will Survive" by Gloria Gaynor comes from my phone, and I curse myself for not changing my ringtone before this trip. How ridiculously lame. I search through my bag, looking for the phone, but by the time I find it, it stops ringing. And then starts again.

"Are you going to answer it or what?" Jordan asks, sounding annoyed.

"Yeah," I say, "as a matter of fact, I am." Which makes no sense, because five seconds ago I wasn't going to answer it, but that was before "I Will Survive" came out of my phone, and now I want Jordan to think I'm fine, and that I just really like seventies disco music. And I know answering my phone will annoy him, which I really, really want to do. This trip is making me mentally exhausted already, and we haven't even crossed state lines.

"Hello!" I say brightly, without checking the caller ID.

"Courtney?" Lloyd asks, sounding like he just woke up.

"Hey," I say, my heart sinking. Lloyd is going to ask even more questions than Jocelyn would have, and there's no way he's going to let me get away with "yes" or "no" answers. It's not that Lloyd is nosey by nature or anything. It's just that he's going to be superconcerned about what's going on with me and Jordan.

"I thought you were going to call me before you left," he says, yawning.

"I was," I say, "but it was so early, I thought I'd let you sleep."

"So how's it going?" he asks. "Are you in the car?" I push the volume down button on my phone, so Jordan won't be able to overhear any of Lloyd's side of the conversation. Who knows what kind of embarrassing things he'll be prone to say.

"Um, yup," I say, "I am." I glance at Jordan out of the corner of my eye. He's staring straight ahead, his hands gripping the steering wheel.

"Is he acting like an asshole?" Lloyd asks.

"Uh, no, not really," I say, as Jordan reaches over and ups the volume on the CD player by about five notches, making it extremely hard to hear Lloyd over the rap music.

"It's probably kind of hard for you to talk right now, huh? With him there and everything?" Ya think?

"Yeah, sort of."

"Okay, well, call me back later. When you're at a rest stop or something."

"I will," I promise.

Lloyd hesitates, like he wants to say something else, but then clicks off.

"Can you please knock it off with the rap?" I say, snapping my cell phone shut and sliding it back into my bag.

"Was that Lloyd?" Jordan asks, trying to sound nonchalant. He's never liked Lloyd, mostly because in the spirit of total relationship honesty, I once made the mistake of telling Jordan about the huge crush I used to have on Lloyd. Have. Had. Shit. The thing is, the first night Jordan and I hung out, I was all set to tell Lloyd that I'd been lusting after him since junior high. And then some, uh, circumstances got in the way, and things didn't work out exactly according to plan.

But then Jordan had to go and dump me for that stupid Internet girl, and Lloyd was being so supportive about the whole thing, and then last night when Lloyd and Jocelyn came over to say good-bye, I was getting all nostalgic, and I started thinking how things would have turned out if I'd never met Jordan. You know, like if Lloyd and I had ended up together. Which was a really stupid thing to start thinking about, since you should never start thinking about "what might have been," and you should also never start thinking about another boy when you're heartbroken over someone else. Although Jocelyn says the only way to get over someone is to get under someone else. So I started thinking maybe that was true, and maybe I needed to date just to get the one "jerk" out of my system, because, let's face it, Jordan was my first real boyfriend, and who ends up with their first real boyfriend? Yeah, no one.

Anyway, to make a long story short, I was feeling nostalgic and Jocelyn left early because she had to have her mom's car home by eleven, and then it was just Lloyd and me, and right before he left he gave me a hug good-bye, and I kissed him. I know. And then, instead of pulling away, he kissed me back, and it turned into this whole big make-out session, and when he left, I started crying, because it turned out that:

a) making out with Lloyd was just weird, and not at all like I thought it would be

b) I should have made out with him sooner, because maybe then I would have gotten over him way before

c) turns out the best way to get over someone is NOT to get under someone else, because after Lloyd left, I missed Jordan more than ever.

Anyway, now it's totally weird, because I don't know what happens next. Especially since Jordan and I are supposed to be stopping in North Carolina tomorrow to visit

Lloyd (he's taking a flight to NC later today), and Jordan's brother, Adam, who also goes to school at Middleton. I suppose at some point Lloyd and I are going to have to talk about our hookup, which is going to be awkward. Or maybe we'll just never mention it again. Stuff like that happens all the time, right? People hook up, and then realize it was a mistake, and since it would be way too awkward to talk about, they just don't.

"What's Lloyd doing up so early?" Jordan asks, smirking.

"Nothing," I snap. I push the eject button on the stereo and pull out the CD that's in the player, which has "Jordan's Gangsta Mix" written on it in black Sharpie. I roll my eyes and replace it with my CD. "Wide Open Spaces" by the Dixie Chicks fills the car, and Jordan rolls his eyes.

"Get used to it," I say, turning back to my book. "We're listening to country."

"Half and half," he says, grinning. "The music on this trip will be fifty-fifty."

"Riiight," I say. "Just like our relationship, right?"

He doesn't say anything, but when we pass the diner, he keeps on driving.

jordan ← before

125 Days Before the Trip, 9:53 p.m.

Courtney McSweeney is grinding on me like she's in a number-one video on *TRL*. I reach around and pull her close to me, our bodies swaying to the music. She looks surprised, but pushes her body harder against mine. She's always so quiet in math. And she definitely doesn't dress like this in school. I catch Madison's eye across the room and quickly look away, as if I've forgotten who she is. I'm not being a dick. Well, okay, maybe I am, but it's only as a means to the end. The end, of course, being getting Madison to hook up with me.

"Hey," I say, pulling away from Courtney. "You want a drink?" She pushes her hair back from her face and smiles.

"Sure." She heads over to where the coolers are and I follow her. Seriously, she really does not dress like this at school. I'm having a very hard time not staring at her ass.

"What do you want to drink?" I ask, rooting through

one of the coolers. The ice makes my hands cold. "There's soda, beer . . . that's it."

"I'll take a beer," she says, sounding unsure. I twist the top off a Corona and hand it to her. She takes a sip.

"So," I say. The music is kind of loud, and I suddenly realize I'm going to now have to be witty and charming so that Courtney looks like she's having a good time, therefore making Madison think I'm flirting with her.

"So," she says. She fiddles with the rim of her beer and looks down at her shoes. Great. So outgoing, this girl.

"Have you started the math assignment yet?" I ask her, figuring it's a safe subject.

"Yeah, I'm actually done with it," she says. I raise my eyebrows and she rushes on. "Just because that's the one grade I'm worried about."

"Really?" I frown. "How come?"

"Calculus is tripping me up for some reason," she says. "So I try to get my stuff done early, and then I have my friend Lloyd look it over. He's this total math genius."

"Sounds like it, with a name like Lloyd." I snort. I'm not trying to be mean, just funny, but she looks hurt. "Whoa," I say. "Just kidding."

"It's okay," she says, looking away. I catch the look on her face, though, which makes me think she's probably sleeping with him. Or wishes she were. "Anyway," she goes on, "I have to keep my math grade up, so I make sure I get the assignments done early so that my friend has time to look them over."

"What's the big deal?" I ask. "Are you wait-listed or something?" Everyone knows the grades we're getting now really have no effect on what happens to us. By now, college applications are finished and sent, and you're either in or you're not. It's a wonder anyone goes to class. I take another sip of my beer and try to pretend I don't notice Madison watching me.

"No," she says. "I'm going to Boston University."

"No shit," I say. "Me, too." Suddenly I have an awful thought. "Are they checking grades for our senior year?"

"I don't know," she says. "I'm just nervous because of that whole thing with the kid from UNC." I give her a blank look. She sighs. "That kid from UNC, you didn't hear about this? He got accepted and then totally blew off all his classes. They withdrew his acceptance since his grades had taken such a turn for the worse."

"I'm sure they were just trying to make an example of him," I say. "I mean, seriously. They're not going to kick you out of BU just because your math grade is bad." I'm not sure if it's true or not, but she strikes me as being the type to worry about every little thing. And I can't have her getting upset. I need to look happy and like I'm this close to getting into her pants, which will therefore make me that much closer to my main goal, which is Madison.

"Anyway," I say, deciding it's time to start making my move. "You're way too cute. All you'd have to do is send them a picture, and I'm sure they wouldn't care if you failed calc." She blushes and I reach out and touch her arm. Out of the corner of my eye, I see Madison set her drink down and start approaching us. Yes. Mission accomplished.

Before she gets there, though, a guy wearing a striped polo shirt—does anyone really wear polo shirts anymore?—approaches Courtney.

"Hey," he says, touching her elbow. "What's goin' on?"

"Hey, Lloyd," she says, her face lighting up. Ah, the infamous Lloyd. He looks like he'd be good in math. But what is he doing here? I mean, besides the obvious partying. Madison picks her drink back up and pretends not to be looking at me. Shit.

"Who's this?" Lloyd asks, sizing me up.

"This is Jordan," Courtney says. "He's in my math class." He's in my math class? How about "I was just grinding on him like I hadn't gotten any in months"? Nice to know where her loyalties are. I take another sip of my beer.

"Hey," Lloyd says, eyeing me. "What's up?"

"Not much, man," I say, wondering when he's going to leave. He's screwing up the plan. I try to look bored in an effort to make him go away. It doesn't work.

"You're still riding home with me, right?" he asks Courtney, watching me out of the corner of his eye. What's with this guy? He looks like he's about one second away from taking a baseball bat to my knees. Or wanting to. I wonder if this is how serial killers start out. Wasn't the Unabomber really good at math?

"Right," Courtney says, glancing at me, too. I take another sip of my Corona. Hey, they don't have to worry about me. The last thing I need is her expecting me to take her home. Like I said, she's cute enough, and her body is smokin', but I have my sights set on something else.

"So, George, are you a junior?" Lloyd asks, and I roll my eyes. What a tool. I know guys like him. Guys who keep a bunch of girls around, dangling themselves in front of them, but never really hooking up with them. Yet they get pissed if someone else tries to make a move. Which I'm not trying to do. But when he calls me George, I almost kind of want to, since I know he knows my name. A not-so-subtle dig. Nice, Lloyd.

"I'm a senior," I say, and leave it at that. There's an awkward silence.

"So, listen," I say, watching Madison out of the corner of my eye. "I need to get back to my friends, but it was nice dancing with you, Court."

"You, too," she says, and for a second, I almost don't do what I'm about to do. Because she seems like a nice girl. But then I see Lloyd giving me the look of death, and I can tell Madison is watching me, so I go for it. Whatever, if I'm going to hell, it will be for hooking up with Kendra Carlson at her brother's graduation party last summer and then never calling her back.

"So, can I get your number?" I say, trying to sound sheepish, like I'm not sure she's going to give it to me. She looks shocked for a minute, so I quickly add, "Oh, I'm sorry, are you two . . ." I look from her to Lloyd, even though I know there's no way they're together. Lloyd's eyes darken. That's what you get for calling me George, Polo Boy.

"Um, no," Courtney says, looking even more flustered.

"No, I can't have your number?" I say, grinning at her again.

"No, we're not together," she says, more forcefully this time. "And yes, you can have my number." Lloyd's eyebrows shoot up in surprise. Did he really think she was going to say no just because of him? It's obvious she wants him, but please. She's not that hard up. Any girl who dances the way she does is not going to sit around waiting for a guy named Lloyd.

Courtney takes a pen and paper out of the small bag slung around her waist and writes her number down. I make a big show out of putting it in my wallet, even though I have no intention of using it. It's mostly so Madison will see me doing it, although later I'll tell her Courtney and I got paired up for a project at school, I was just dancing with her to be nice, and I got her number so we could work on the assignment. She won't know whether it's true or not, but again, that's part of the fun.

"Nice to meet you, Lloyd," I say, looking right at him. "And I'll give ya a call," I say to Courtney.

"Later," she says, and I think briefly about what's going to happen at school on Monday when I blow her off.

Thankfully, she sits on the other side of the room in math class. And she doesn't seem psychotic, which is always a plus. Psychotic girls are a pain in my ass. Last year I kissed this freshman girl at a pool party and she wouldn't get off my nuts for six months. Which is why my policy is now no psychotics, and no freshmen. The freshmen thing is obviously easy to avoid, while the psychotics pose a bit more of a problem. It's not like girls walk around with "I'm crazy" stamped on their chests.

I decide to head around the party the long way, and then sneak up on Madison from behind. How cute would that be, me doing to her the same trick she pulled earlier? But when I make my way through the crowd to where Madison and her friends were standing, the only one there is B. J. His leprechaun hat is stained with beer and he's sitting on the ground, looking dejected.

"Dude," I say, crouching down next to him. "You okay?"

"Yeah," he says mournfully. "I'm okay. I'm just drunk."

"Sucks."

"Yeah," he agrees.

"Hey, you didn't happen to notice where Madison Allesio and her friends went, did you?"

"I'm not sure," he says, looking thoughtful. He frowns, pulls his leprechaun hat off his head, and twists it in his hands. "I think they said something about going to Jeremy Norfolk's house." Shit. Jeremy Norfolk was also having a party tonight, and apparently Madison and her friends took off while they were supposed to be waiting for me. I'm impressed in spite of myself, and a little bit turned on. Any girl who ditches me while I'm in the process of trying to make her jealous is hot.

"You want to head over to Jeremy's?" I ask B. J. He looks at me, his eyes glazed over and the front of his leprechaun outfit soaked in beer.

"Yes." He nods.

"Dude, you're shot," I say. "You're not going anywhere but home. Come on." I try to help B. J. up without actually getting too close to him. No way I want to kick it to Madison smelling like drunk leprechaun.

Twenty minutes later, after getting B. J. some drive-thru coffee and bringing him home, I decide to stop at my house to reapply my cologne and kill some time. I can't have Madison thinking I took off after her as soon as I realized she was gone.

There's an unfamiliar car in my driveway. My dad's out of town, so I'm assuming it's one of my mom's clients—she's a lawyer, and sometimes when she's in the middle of a big case, she'll have clients over to the house. I open the glove compartment and take a piece of gum out, popping it into my mouth just in case I smell like alcohol. I only had a couple of beers, but the last thing I need is to look drunk and disorderly in front of my mom and one of her clients.

"Mom!" I call, moving through the foyer, and trying to calculate how long my mom might be up and working. She's a heavy sleeper, and our house is big enough that if my mom's asleep, I could totally bring Madison back here with me later on. "I'm home."

I hear some scuffling and whispers coming from the living room. I turn the corner, and that's when I see it. My mom. On the couch, with her shirt unbuttoned. There's some guy next to her, with his shirt OFF. And it's not my dad. For a second, I just stand there.

"Jordan," my mom says, smoothing her hair. She pulls her shirt closed. "I didn't think you'd be home until much later."

"Obviously," I say, sizing up the guy she's with. He doesn't look embarrassed. Instead, he looks almost pleased. No one moves. We all just wait, not saying anything.

"It's okay," I finally say. I turn around and head back toward the door. "I was actually going back out anyway, so . . ." I trail off, not really sure what I'm supposed to say.

"You don't have to," the guy says. He stands up from the couch. "I was just leaving anyway."

"I know I don't HAVE to," I say, turning back around. "I live here."

"Jordan—" my mom starts, but I turn on my heel and head out to my car. I slam the door of my truck and turn the music up. Loud. I sit there for a second, expecting my mom to come rushing out after me, to explain, to tell me it was some weird misunderstanding. But she doesn't.

After a few minutes, I turn the music down and back out of the driveway. I have no idea where I'm going or what I'm going to do. I'm so not in the mood to chase Madison anymore, and B. J.'s definitely done for the night. And all my other friends are probably at Jeremy's party. I drive around aimlessly for a few minutes, and then I remember Courtney McSweeney's number, written on a piece of paper in my wallet.

courtney ← before

125 Days Before the Trip, 11:37 p.m.

So I chickened out. About telling Lloyd, I mean. But it wasn't really my fault, because while we were leaving the party, we ran into Olivia Meacham outside, and she was all over Lloyd in one of those "I'm making it clear you can have sex with me if you want" kind of ways. Which I could never figure out. How girls can do that, I mean. I'm always terrified of giving a guy any idea I might like him, so I overcompensate by acting like I don't. Like tonight, for example. I totally wanted to dance with Jordan. But I hesitated because:

    a) I thought I would look stupid. Which I probably did, but hopefully everyone was too drunk to notice.
    b) I didn't want him to think I wanted him. Because I don't. I want Lloyd. But the point is, no matter who it is, a guy I don't like or a guy I do, I don't want them to think I like them.

Anyway. There was Olivia Meacham, wearing a frayed denim skirt that I'd tried on once in Hollister with Jocelyn and then vetoed because it was way too short, and a blue halter top that showed off her stomach. It's taken me, oh, I don't know, five years to get up the courage to even *think* about telling Lloyd I like him. Olivia transferred into our school around Christmas, and three months later she's practically going down on him at this party.

Anyway, Lloyd starting flirting with Olivia, and the next thing I knew, she was in the car with us, and Lloyd was giving us both a ride home. And Lloyd dropped me off first. Which was kind of weird, since he made that whole production out of making sure I was riding home with him, when that wasn't even the plan to begin with. But I'm not stupid. I know you always drop the third wheel off first.

So here I am, at home, by myself, and it's kind of this big letdown. I really did want to tell him. And I can't even bitch about it to Jocelyn, because she's not answering her phone or replying to my text messages.

And of course no one's on instant messenger, because everyone's either sleeping or out. I download a few songs from iTunes, and then decide to see if Jordan has a MySpace. Not because I like him or anything. But because I'm curious.

"Jordan Richman," I type into the search bar, and his profile pops up on the screen. The song he's chosen is "Let's All Get Drunk Tonight" by Afroman. Charming. I scroll through his pics. One of him at school, hanging out in the quad, one of him with his brother, Adam, who I recognize because he was a senior when we were freshman. And a bunch of Jordan with girls. Seriously, he has like ten pics of him with girls. Don't the girls get mad? I wonder. That they're on his page with a bunch of other girl pics?

I hit the back button and check out his friends. 789 friends. Quite the popular one, that Jordan. I have 117.

I scroll through the comments.

Seems like he and "Mad Madd Madison" have quite the MySpace flirtation going on. I go back and forth between their profiles, reading them. "What are you wearing?" Jordan asked her. "Why don't you come over and I'll show you," Madison wrote back. Gag. They couldn't come up with anything better than that? How lame.

My cell phone rings, and I reach for it, figuring it's Jocelyn calling me back. But the caller ID shows a number I don't recognize.

"Hello?"

"Court?"

"This is Courtney," I say, cradling the phone between my shoulder and chin and scrolling through Madison's pictures, most of which show her pouting for the camera, and wearing bathing suits. Seriously, bathing suits. And she's not in the beach or by the pool in any of them.

"Hey," the voice says, sounding nervous. "It's Jordan."

"Oh," I say. "Um, hi." I close out the browser, wondering

if he somehow saw I was on his profile, and is now calling to tell me to stop stalking him.

"You weren't sleeping, were you?"

"No, not at all," I say. "I just got home a little while ago."

"Cool," he says, and there's a pause.

"So, uh, what are you doing? Home from the party?" Oh, yeah, that was really great. Obviously he's home from the party, or he wouldn't be calling me. This is why I've never had a boyfriend. Because while other girls are wearing halter tops and leaving flirtatious messages on people's MySpace profiles, I'm coming up with such gems as "So, uh, what are you doing?"

"Driving around," he says. "I dropped B. J. off and then I was going to hit this other party, but I'm not really in the mood."

"Cool," I say. "But why are you driving around at" — I glance at the clock — "midnight?"

"I'm not sure," he says, sounding confused. "Just seemed fitting."

"Um, okay," I say.

"So," he says. "Where do you live?"

"Where do I live?" I say, flopping down on my bed. "Jordan, I can't tell you that! Technically, you're a stranger."

"I'm not a stranger," he says. "And besides, if I don't know where you live, I can't pick you up."

"Pick me up?" I say, swallowing.

"Yeah," he says. "So you can come to breakfast with me."

"How do you know I'm hungry?" I ask, thinking about his MySpace profile pics, and wondering if all those girls were invited to breakfast, too. I wonder if it's one of those weird competitions guys have. Like this one thing I read about guys in college who made up this game to see who could sleep with the biggest girl. It was really, really mean. Disgusting. Maybe Jordan and his friends have some sort of twisted MySpace pics competition. If he thinks he's getting a pic of us together, he's wrong.

"Well, are you?"

"Starved, actually." I *am* hungry. But that doesn't mean I'm going to breakfast with him. I mean, hello? Isn't this how people get stalked and killed? They sneak out in the middle of the night to meet some guy they know nothing about, and the next thing you know, no one ever hears from them again.

"So it's all settled," he says. "Where do you live?"

I hesitate.

"Courtney?" he says. "Please?" And there's something in the way he says my name that makes me think he really, really wants me to come.

I sigh and reach for the jeans lying on my floor. "Twelve thirty-five Whickam Way," I say. "And you better be buying."

"That was so good," I say an hour later, pushing my plate away. "I can't believe I ate all that at one in the morning. Definitely not a good idea."

"Ahh, it's fine," he says. He reaches over and uses his fork to cut a piece of the pancake that's left on my plate. He pops it in his mouth.

"How can you possibly want to eat any more?" I say. He's had three of his own pancakes, piled high with strawberries and whipped cream, three pieces of bacon, three sausages, home fries, and now he's eating what's left of mine.

"I'm hungry." He shrugs and picks up the check, which the waitress has left on our table. He pulls out a twenty from his wallet.

"How much do I owe?" I ask. I reach into my bag and rummage for my wallet.

"Nah," he says. "Don't worry about it."

"No," I say. "Absolutely not. I'm not letting you pay."

"Why not?" he asks, cutting himself another piece of pancake. "I forced you out of your house at midnight, it's the least I can do."

"You didn't force me," I say.

He shrugs. "Well, whatever. I'm paying."

"Thanks," I say, sliding my wallet back into my bag, and suddenly feeling awkward. I know I joked with him on the phone about him paying, but still. Does this mean it's a date? Who goes on a date at midnight with some guy she met at a party? It's very weird. Is this how things work? Do girls just pick up guys randomly and then go on dates with them? I guess so, since Olivia Meacham hooked Lloyd tonight in about two seconds. Although technically, Jordan picked me up, not the other way around.

"So," Jordan says, standing up. "What do you want to do now?"

"What do I want to do now? Um, in case you haven't noticed, it's one in the morning."

"So?" he says, grinning. "It's early. Oh, unless your parents need to have you home or something."

"Oh, no," I say. "It's nothing like that." The truth is, my parents would probably be thrilled that I'm out. My dad, especially. He's always trying to get me to go out more, instead of just sitting at home, doing homework or playing around on my computer. "My parents totally trust me," I tell Jordan. I reach over and take a sip of my hot chocolate, then grab two sugars from the container on the table and dump them into my cup. "It comes from being such a Goody Two-shoes for the first eighteen years of my life. They refuse to believe that I could do anything wrong, so they pretty much let me do whatever I want."

"So you've built their trust to a point where they wouldn't even consider the idea that their daughter could be text messaging when she's supposed to be learning about cosines, right?"

I almost spit out my coffee. "Hey," I say, "how did you know about that?" I spend almost all of math class texting to Jocelyn, since she has unstructured that period. I usually have a handle on the math stuff from reading the chapters the night before, and plus Lloyd goes over all my work, so it's not like I'm really missing out on anything. But how does Jordan know this?

"I'm at the perfect angle to see you pull out your phone," he says, grinning. "You do it all covert, hiding it under the pocket of your hoodie. Which, by the way, you always put on right before calc, so that you can text."

"Everyone texts in class," I say, shrugging my shoulders. It feels weird knowing he was watching me, that he knows something about me. Thank God he doesn't know exactly what I'm texting Jocelyn about, because trust me, he would flip out. Let's just say the words "Lloyd" and "sex" are used a lot. Not that I'm having sex with Lloyd. Or want to. I just like to talk about it. A lot.

"Anyway," I say, as the waitress comes by and drops the change onto our table, "thanks for breakfast." Jordan leaves $5 on the table and puts the rest of the money back in his wallet. So he's a big tipper. That's hot.

"So what do you want to do now?" Jordan asks, standing up.

"What do I want to do now?" I say. I check my watch. "Well, seeing as we're under twenty-one, I'm thinking our choices are home or home."

"Super Wal-Mart is open," Jordan says, holding open the door for me. "And I heard they're having a sale on hoodies. You could get another one. You know, to help you in math."

"Oh, yeah, great plan," I say. "Our first date you take me out to breakfast at one a.m., and then to Super Wal-Mart. How romantic." He looks uncomfortable for a second. "Not that this is a date or anything," I add quickly. "I was just messing around." Oh, my God, could I have been any dumber? Who says that? Refers to a random call from a guy she doesn't even know at one in the morning as a date? It's so not a date. Dates are when the guy calls you days in advance to set something up, and shows up at your house, meets your parents, and then takes you somewhere. And everyone knows that you're not supposed to even accept a date for the weekend after a Wednesday, because then you supposedly look desperate, right? Or is it Thursday? Whatever; the point is, this is so not a date. In fact, I'm not sure what it is. If I didn't know any better, I'd say it was a booty call. Booty calls always happen at one in the morning. But with booty calls, aren't you supposed to get right to it? Like, the point of the booty call is to get naked right away, not mess around with formalities like dinner and dates. Unless this is a booty call, and I just don't know it. And Jordan is trying to trick me into getting naked by taking me out to breakfast first, so then later, when I'm like, "That was a booty call!" he can be like, "No, it wasn't, we had breakfast." Like a modified booty call. It's probably the new trend in dating.

"So," Jordan says once we're on the road. "You really have to go home?"

"Yeah," I say, thinking about the MySpace comments

him and Mad Maddy exchanged less than twenty-four hours ago. "I should really get home." For a second, I expect that he's going to try to convince me to come back to his place, or worse, park the car in the Super Wal-Mart parking lot so we can mess around. I mean, why else would he invite me out? Like I said, it's not a date, and if it's not a booty call, then what the hell?

He pulls into my driveway. "Are you sure you live here?" he asks, sliding the car into park, but leaving the engine running.

"I'm pretty sure," I say. I pull my keys out of my purse. "I have a key and everything."

"It's just that the mailbox says 'Brewster,' and your last name is McSweeney. So I need to make sure you're not involved in any illegal activity, where I might be implicated since we hung out tonight."

"What sort of illegal activity?" I ask. "Breaking into people's houses to sleep?"

"Well, it could be anything," he says, leaning back in his seat and pretending to look thoughtful. "This could be the headquarters for your drug trafficking posse. And all that texting you do in math is business related, and must be done during eighth period because of the time difference in certain South American countries."

"Yeah, I'm a total drug trafficker," I say, rolling my eyes. "I'm surprised your friend B. J. hasn't told you about me — he's my biggest client."

"Touché," Jordan says, grinning.

"No, but seriously, the truth isn't anything all that shady," I say, looking away for a second. "I have a different last name than my parents."

"Oh," he says. "I'm somewhat disappointed that it's something so normal."

"Maybe I'll tell you about it sometime," I say, opening the door. Although if you want to know the truth, I don't really want to leave. Which is crazy. I mean, this is Jordan Richman. He is totally not my type. Actually, I'm not his type. He likes girls like Olivia and Madison, girls that are super confident around guys and have the hookup list to back it up. My hookup list reads like this:

1. Kissed Jocelyn's cousin Justin during her seventh-grade birthday party during a game of spin the bottle. He had greasy lips. No tongue was involved.

2. Ninth grade—went on two dates with Paul Gilmore (once to the movies and once to dinner at the restaurant his dad owns, which I'm not sure really counts, since he didn't have to pay). Made out (kissing with tongue) during each date, which was slightly awkward since once we were in a movie theater, and once we were in the kitchen of his dad's restaurant.

3. Spent some of last year hooking up with Blake Letkowski, even though he was never really my boyfriend. He smoked. He was bad news. But he was a really good kisser.

Jordan unbuckles his seat belt and turns off the car. "Let me walk you to the door," he says.

"Oh, no, that's okay," I say, hopping out before he can protest. The last thing I want is some random awkward moment at my door, where he's trying to weasel his way into my house so he can attempt to devirginize me. I turn around and look back at him in the car. "Thanks again for breakfast, Jordan."

"My pleasure," he says.

"So, um, see you in school on Monday," I say, realizing it's true. I will see him in school on Monday. Which is weird. Thinking about seeing him in school, I mean.

"See you," he says, and I slam the car door. He waits until I'm safely inside before starting his car back up and pulling out of my driveway. I watch him from my living room window, wondering what the hell just happened, and how I ended up going out to breakfast with Jordan Richman.

courtney | the trip

Day One, 11:56 a.m.

We haven't said a word to each other for the past two hours. I'm starving, but I can't really admit it now, since I pitched such a fit about not wanting to eat before. But really, I could go for a burger. A huge one, dripping with mayonnaise and ketchup. I've been turning pages of *The Catcher in the Rye* for the past two hours without actually reading any of it. I know, how lame. The good thing is that since I've read the book so many times, it doesn't matter, because I already know what's going on.

My mix CD is still playing. This is the third time it's repeated, and even I'm getting sick of the songs. But I figure if Jordan's making an effort to be nice, I'm not going to turn it off. I mean, it's either listening to these over and over or putting rap on, and that's so not going to happen.

It's kind of strange, being in the car and not saying anything to each other. It's like some kind of suspense movie.

Or like being in an alternate universe, where we're not really Jordan and Courtney, but some other people who don't talk to each other.

My stomach grumbles really loudly, and I see Jordan smirk. But not in a mean way. More in a "isn't that cute" kind of way. For a second, I feel a pang in my stomach, almost like I'm going to cry, but then I start to get a little mad. He doesn't have the right to make a "isn't she so cute" face at me.

"Whatever," I say. "Like your stomach never grumbled."

"It's just funny," he says.

"I don't see why."

"Because you're obviously hungry, and yet you haven't said anything because you're afraid to not stick to the itinerary, because if we go off it even a little bit, you'll think you'll have 'lost' or something. And you hate to lose."

"That's not true," I say, even though it totally is. Well, sort of. It's not that I think I'll have lost, it's just I don't want to give him the satisfaction of thinking he was right. Besides, the itinerary says we're going to stop in another hour and a half, and I can certainly wait until then. I just won't think about it. La, la, la. Not thinking about burgers.

"It is true," he says matter-of-factly. "You'd rather starve than give me the satisfaction."

"Whatever," I say. "I'm not hungry at all."

Two minutes later, he pulls into a rest stop. "There," he says, putting the car in park. "Now technically you didn't give in, and yet we can still eat." He smiles, his brown eyes sparkling. "And I'm hungry, too."

I'm about to protest, but instead I just pull my seat belt off and slide out of the car. I feel like I want to cry again, which is so, so, ridiculous. I mean, it's not like we were even together that long. Four months is nothing. Four months is like, less than a lot of those reality TV shows. And those people live together. And then probably never talk again. Plus, what about people who get divorced? Like people who are married for ten or fifteen years, and then never speak again? Some of them even go on to get married to other people. And then someone's like, "Hey, whatever happened to your first husband, Harry?" And they're like, "Oh, Harry, yeah, I forgot about him. I'm not sure. I think he might be running a casino in Vegas." People come and go, in and out of each other's lives like it's nothing. So I don't know how/why this should be a big deal.

I follow Jordan into the rest stop, which is really quite awkward. I can't walk next to him, because that's very, you know, couple like, but walking behind him is weird, too, because then it's like I'm not walking next to him on purpose, which may lead him to believe that he's actually affecting me, which I definitely don't want. For him to be affecting me, I mean. Or, for him to think that. Because he obviously *is* affecting me.

When we get inside, he heads to the Burger King line, and I go to Sbarro. I actually wanted Burger King, too, but there's no way I was going to stand in that wicked long line with him while we tried to make conversation. Or worse, just stood there in silence. I brought my book in with me, so hopefully while we're eating, I can read and he can just eat and look at the ground.

I order a sausage calzone before I realize that I should probably get the grilled chicken salad, since now that I have no boyfriend, I need to make sure I don't get really fat. I've been eating a lot lately, and with the freshman fifteen probably a given, I need to make sure I at least make some kind of effort to eat healthy. If I didn't know better, I would have started to think I was pregnant, what with all the food I've been eating. But I know I'm not, because Jordan and I never actually did it. The only time we came close was in Miami, right before we broke up. Thinking about that night makes me feel sick, and I almost throw my sausage calzone into a nearby trash can on my way to pick a table. But then I realize that if I don't have any food, Jordan's going to wonder why, and then what will I say? "Because I'm too upset about you dumping me to eat." I don't think so.

Despite the long Burger King line, Jordan's already sitting at a table when I get there, and so I slide in across from him.

"Hey," he says, unwrapping his Whopper. "What'd you get?"

"Sausage calzone," I say, putting the straw into my diet Coke. I reach into my bag and pull out my book.

"You're kidding, right?" Jordan says, raising his eyebrows.

"No," I say. "I really did get a sausage calzone." Why would I kid about that?

"I mean the book," he says. He takes a bite of his burger and licks his lips. I look away quickly, because a wave of heat has started between my legs and is now moving its way up my body. How ridiculous. That I'm getting turned on just from watching him lick his lips. Especially since he's such an asshole.

"What about it?"

"You're going to read your book at lunch?"

"Yeah, that was the plan," I say.

"Lame," he says, shrugging. He takes the top off his soda and takes a big drink. Jordan never uses a straw. He says it's because he can't get enough soda that way. I used to think it was cute. Apparently I still do, because I'm still getting hot just looking at him.

"Why is it lame?" I ask, frowning.

"It's just kind of rude." He shrugs again.

"Yeah, I don't think we should get into a conversation about what's rude and what isn't," I say. "Or who's ruder. Because I have a feeling I'd win that argument." He shifts in his chair uncomfortably. Good. I cut a piece of my calzone and pop it into my mouth. I look down at my book and try to concentrate on the words.

Suddenly Jordan's cell phone starts playing "Baby Got Back" again. He checks the caller ID, frowns, and then sends it to voice mail without answering it.

"Don't not answer it on account of me," I say. "It doesn't bother me at all."

"I thought it did," he says. "In the car, you acted like it did."

"Well, it doesn't here," I say, chewing and swallowing, even though the calzone tastes funny in my mouth. "In the car, you shouldn't talk on your phone, but here, it's okay. Besides, I'm reading." I force down another bite of calzone, and turn a page in my book.

"It wasn't important," he says.

"Whatever." I shrug.

"If it was, I would have answered it," he says. He takes another bite of his burger. And licks his lips again. My stomach does a flip.

"Good," I say. "Because I would hope that you wouldn't not answer a call from your girlfriend just because of me." Shit. Shit, shit, shit. Why would I say that? Why would I bring up the dreaded *G* word? It reverberates around us, like an echo. Girlfriend, girlfriend, girlfriend. We've never talked about his new girlfriend. Actually, since we broke up, we haven't really talked at all. Okay, stay calm. La, la, la, pretending I didn't say anything.

"It wasn't my girlfriend," he says, looking right at me. I practice making my face a complete blank. Like I'm in one of those poker tournaments and there's a million dollars on the line, and if my face betrays my emotions, then I'll lose it all. I look straight ahead. Think of things that don't make me emotional. Um. Spanish tests. Baseball. Pink shoes. Actually, I love pink shoes.

"Oh," I say, because someone has to say something. "I just want you to know that you don't have to not answer it because of me. If, you know, she does end up calling." I am so smooth.

"Thanks," he says, looking confused. "Aren't you hungry?" He looks at my sausage calzone, and since I don't want him to think I've lost my appetite from thinking about his skanky girlfriend, I down the whole thing even though it tastes disgusting. The sausage is rubbery, and the cheese tastes like plastic.

"Wow," Jordan says. "You really were hungry."

"Yup," I say, taking a big sip of my drink. "Good calzone." Not.

And then I do something that is so totally ridiculous, but I can't stop myself. It's one of those things that you know you shouldn't do, but you have to. Kind of like at the prom, when I had spent fifty dollars to get my nails done (those really cute acrylics that look real if you get the expensive kind), and while Jocelyn and I were in the bathroom reapplying our lipstick, one of my nails seemed a little loose, so I pried it off with a nail file. It was a really stupid idea, because I had to go around for the rest of the week with one nail missing. But I couldn't stop myself. And that's how it is right now.

"So," I say, "how are things going? You know, with, um, your girlfriend?" I try to say it like I'm asking because I want him to be happy, but I'm afraid it comes out more like I'm prying. Since I just downed my whole calzone, I take a sip of my soda so I'll appear nonchalant.

"Fine," he says, shifting in his seat.

"Good," I say. "I'm glad." My stomach lurches, and I don't know if it's all the greasy food or the fact that I'm thinking about Jordan with another girl.

"Yeah," Jordan says. "And, uh, I guess, you and Lloyd?"

"What?" I say.

"You and Lloyd," he says. "You guys are like a thing now?"

"Yeah," I say, "we're a thing now." Oh. My. God. I cannot believe I just said that. Me and Lloyd are so not a thing. Well, I guess we're as much of a thing as you can be when you make out with someone in your room. Oh, my God. Am I slut? I think I'm a slut. I mean, who lets some random guy go up their shirt when they're in love with someone else? Not that Lloyd is really all that random. I mean, I've known him forever. And lusted after him for just as long. So maybe it was good that I got it out of my system. Because like I said, hooking up with Lloyd was . . . strange. But maybe that's just because we weren't used to each other. I don't really have much to compare it to, except for Jordan. And the first night he and I hooked up was weird, because it was so random. But then it got better. The hooking up, I mean. Because we got used to each other. Maybe Lloyd and I just have to get used to each other?

"Wait," I say. "How'd you know that Lloyd and I were a thing?"

"B. J. told me," he says.

"How does B. J. know?" I ask, rubbing my temples with my fingers. I'm starting to feel light-headed. Is this how celebrities feel, having their secrets splashed across the tabloids and wondering how the hell everyone found out?

"I guess Lloyd left some kind of comment on your MySpace profile," Jordan says, shrugging, "that led B. J. to believe you two were a thing."

I haven't checked my MySpace since last night, before I let Lloyd grope me. Although it wasn't really groping. It was more like . . . I dunno, stroking? Eww, that sounds so nasty. And it wasn't. Nasty, I mean. It just wasn't amazing, like it is with Jordan. Lloyd was kind of tentative, like he wasn't sure what he was doing. Not like I do. Know what I'm doing, exactly. Besides, you'd think that Lloyd would have taken the lead, since I know for a fact he's not a virgin and I am. Although not by my choice. I start thinking about that night in Miami with Jordan again and I really do feel dizzy.

"What did it say?" I ask, trying to make the room stop spinning.

"What did what say?" Jordan asks, frowning. He takes the last bite of his burger and licks his lips again. Can he STOP DOING THAT? Really, how much can one person lick his lips?

"What did the MySpace comment say?" I take a small sip of soda in an effort to calm my stomach down. Isn't that what soda is supposed to do? Make your stomach calm down? Actually, I think that's just ginger ale. Flat ginger ale.

"You don't know?"

"I haven't been online since last night," I say. "My laptop was already packed." I mean it to come out as kind of a dig, like I was all packed up and he wasn't, but it comes out like I'm panicked.

"I'm not sure." Jordan shrugs, and balls up the paper that his Whopper was wrapped in. He's not sure? He's not sure? That's ridiculous. How can he not be sure? As soon as B. J. was like, "Lloyd left Courtney a MySpace comment and I think they're a thing," Jordan should have been like, "Why, what did it say?" That's what I would have done.

"Oh." My stomach is on fire now, but I'm ignoring it. "Well," I say, standing up. I stretch my arms over my head like I don't have a care in the world. "I'm going to the bathroom, and then we'll get back on the road, sound good?"

"Sure." He stands up and starts to gather the trash from our table and put it on the tray. I walk toward the rest rooms, but as soon as I'm out of Jordan's sight, I pull out my cell and dial Jocelyn.

"Hello," she says, sounding groggy.

"Hi!" I say. "It's me."

"Oh," she says. There's a muffled noise on the line, like she's rolling over.

"Are you sleeping?" I say.

"Yes," she mumbles.

"Oh," I say. "Well, listen, I need you to do something for me."

"What?"

"You need to check my MySpace page for me." I look over my shoulder, fearful Jordan might head for the bathrooms when he's done picking up the garbage and see me standing outside, talking on my cell. I walk quickly toward the bathrooms just in case, figuring I can talk as easily in there and not arouse suspicion.

"Now?" Jocelyn asks, sighing. "Honey, no one has left you any comments this morning, trust me. It's too early for that." She yawns.

"It was last night," I say. "Lloyd left me a comment last night."

"What?!" she screeches, sounding fully awake. I hear another mumbled noise, and then the sound of her computer booting up. "What does it say?"

"I don't know," I say, trying not to become exasperated with her, since she's my one link to the Internet. "That's why I'm asking you to check." There's a line at the bathroom that stretches out the door and into the hallway, and I fall into it, behind a woman and her baby. She has a pink streak in her hair. The woman, not the baby.

"How do you know he left you a comment?" she asks gleefully. "Court, this is so hot, what do you think it says?"

"I don't know," I say. My stomach starts churning again. "Probably just like, 'Hey, had fun hanging out with you tonight,' or something like that."

"Maybe it has to do with you going to see him tomorrow," she says. "What time does his flight leave today?"

"I think one this afternoon," I say. "He was supposed to get to Middleton at around three or four."

"Just fyi, I think it's kind of corny that you guys are stopping to visit him," she says. "I mean, he'll have been at college for one day. Could you be any more desperate?"

"I'm not going just to see him," I say. "Jordan is going to see his brother, and Lloyd just happened to find out about it, and decided it would be cool to meet up." Jordan's brother, Adam, is going to be a senior at the University of Middleton, and he stayed in North Carolina this summer to do an internship. When Lloyd found out we were stopping on our way to Boston, he thought it would be cool if we could get together so I'd have a chance to see where he was going to school.

"But he invited you before you guys hooked up, right?" Jocelyn asks. "So it was like a friend thing."

"Oh, my God," I say. "Maybe Lloyd realizes hooking up was a huge mistake, and he doesn't want me to come anymore. Maybe his MySpace comment says something like, 'Wow, I can't believe I was so horny that that happened tonight, but I hope you didn't read anything into it. Maybe it's not a great idea for you to come visit after all.'"

"No," Jocelyn says, her voice low and even, like she's talking to some kind of mental patient. "Because B. J. told Jordan that Lloyd's comment made it seem like you guys were a thing."

Oh. Right. I take a deep breath.

"Okay," Jocelyn says. "It's loading. Hold on, I'm typing your page in." The sound of keystrokes comes over the line. "Okay, let's see . . . Oh, here it is."

"What does it say?" I almost scream. The old woman two people ahead of me in line turns around and gives me a dirty look.

"Don't freak out," she says, which is never good, because if someone has to preface what they're saying with "Don't freak out," you're probably going to freak out.

"Just. Read. It," I say.

"Okay." She clears her throat like she's about to give an oral presentation. "It says, 'Hey, beautiful. I had the best time with you tonight—seriously, it was amazing. I can't wait to see you tomorrow and talk about what this means. Thank goodness for frequent flyer miles, right? Sleep well, Courtney Elizabeth.'"

For a moment, I can't speak. Lloyd obviously does think we're a thing. Which we most certainly aren't. Which means that tomorrow, I am going to have to tell him we're *not* a thing, while trying to make it out to

Jordan that we *are* a thing, since I just told him we were.

"Court?" Jocelyn's saying. "Are you there?"

"Yeah, I'm here," I say. And then, before I can get into the bathroom, I throw up all over the floor.

courtney ← before

123 Days Before the Trip, 12:23 p.m.

"No," Jocelyn says, taking a sip of her chocolate milk and regarding me over the cafeteria table. "That's not going to happen."

"What isn't?" I ask, trying to sound innocent. I've just finished telling Jocelyn about my night with Jordan, and she's acting like it's this huge, bad idea. Which it probably is. But only if I like him. Which I don't.

"You are not going to start pining away for Jordan Richman," she says. "I won't let it happen."

"I'm not pining away for him!" I say. I open up the packet of blue cheese dressing that came with my salad and pour it over the lettuce on my plate. I'm not even really that hungry, but I need something to keep myself busy, so that I don't betray the way I'm feeling, which is that I may have a crush on Jordan. Which is insane. Because Jocelyn is right. That's just ridiculous.

"Good," Jocelyn says, looking satisfied. She takes another sip of her soda, then reaches over and grabs a cucumber off my salad. She pops it into her mouth. "But it is a little weird that he called you like that." She frowns. "Although it's even weirder that he didn't try anything."

"What do you mean?" I ask.

"Well, it's just that if a guy calls you late at night like that, usually it means he wants something physical. So for him not to try anything is kind of weird, you know?"

"Unless he thought he wanted to hook up with me, and then when he sobered up, he found me repulsive and decided not to."

"Was he drinking?"

"Not really."

Jocelyn rolls her eyes. "Then that makes no sense. Anyway, why are we still talking about this?"

"I have no idea." Because I can't stop thinking about him, and was a little disappointed when he didn't call me yesterday. Okay, even I can see that's pretty ridiculous. I mean, he's not my boyfriend. He's not even a guy I'm dating. So to be disappointed that he didn't call me on Sunday is just stupid. I think I should chalk it up to a random thing, one of those freak occurrences that no one can really explain. Like crop circles. Or that lady who got hit by a foul ball at a Yankees game, and then when she went to get it checked out, it turned out they found a tumor, and if she hadn't gotten it checked out, she would have died.

"Good," Jocelyn says, sounding satisfied.

"But . . ." I say slowly, twirling a piece of lettuce around on my fork.

"But what?" Jocelyn screeches. "There are no buts!" She grabs my hand and stops me from twirling. "Honey, no," she instructs. "He's bad news. He's not right for you."

"I know," I say. "You're right. Definitely." I frown. The thing is, when we were hanging out, he *did* seem right for me. Nothing like I really thought he was. But maybe that's just a ploy, something he does to make girls want him. It makes sense when you think about it—he must be doing *something* to get all these girls to fall in love with him. It must have to do with sweet-talking them and making them think he's a good guy. But I will not fall for that. I will be strong and not give into his psychotic, mind game–playing ways.

"Don't talk to him anymore," Jocelyn says. "Don't look at him, don't call him, don't online stalk him."

"I won't," I say, not mentioning the fact that I checked his MySpace profile about three hundred times yesterday, and was secretly very pleased to see that Madison Allesio left him a comment, which he never replied to.

"I mean it, Courtney," she says. "Don't go getting all psychotic over something that's not even a thing."

"You're totally right," I say. And she is. Getting all worked up over some guy who is definitely not a thing is really stupid. Especially since I'm already all worked up over Lloyd, who is also not a thing, and is even hooking up with the girl he met at Connor's party. Unlike Jordan, Lloyd did call me yesterday, to tell me about how he felt up Olivia in the backseat of his car. Things in my love life are not going well.

"Besides, what about Lloyd?" Jocelyn asks, like she's reading my mind. She picks a cherry tomato off my plate and puts it in her mouth. I wordlessly hand her my fork, and she spears a forkful of my salad. Jocelyn is one of those people who is always trying to lose weight by not eating and then makes up for it by eating off everyone else's plate.

"He's hooking up with Olivia."

"Lame," Jocelyn says, rolling her eyes. "I give it a couple weeks."

"Yeah, maybe," I say. Madison Allesio goes walking by, flanked on both sides by girls from her cheerleading squad. I swallow hard.

"I have a scandal going on," Jocelyn announces.

"Oh, God," I say. "Do I even want to know?"

"Yes," Jocelyn says. "You want to know." She bites her lip. "But you can't get mad at me for not telling you sooner." Jocelyn likes to sit on her scandals. As in, she likes to wait a few days before telling anyone what's going on. Last year when she broke up with Kevin Scott, who she'd been dating for two years, she didn't tell me for a week. I just thought they were in a big fight, since I didn't see them hanging around each other in school. I've learned not to take it too personally. It's just how she is.

"I won't," I say. I wonder if the fact that Jordan Richman called me out of nowhere on the same night I was supposed to tell Lloyd I wanted him is some kind of sign. That Jordan and I are supposed to be together. Or that Lloyd and I aren't. Or that I really am supposed to be with Lloyd. That last one makes no sense, though, because why would Lloyd hooking up with Olivia mean he and I are supposed to be together? This is why believing in signs is never a good idea. They're so damn confusing.

"Okay," she says. "You know how on Saturday night you tried calling me really late, but I didn't answer?"

"Yes," I say. Unlike Jocelyn, I like to dissect and analyze any drama I'm involved in immediately. As soon as I got home from hanging out with Jordan on Saturday night, I called her.

"And you know how I didn't answer?" she says.

"Yes."

"And you know how I didn't call you back until four in the morning?"

"Yes," I say.

"And you know how you said you were sleeping, but we talked anyway, because—"

"Jocelyn! Yes, I know, I was there, now spill."

"Well," she says slowly. She twirls a strand of her light brown hair around her finger. "It was because I was hooking up with someone."

"Really?" I say. "Was it Mark?"

"No," she says.

I wait. Silence.

"Okay," I say. "Are you going to tell me who it was?"

"I don't know," she says.

"Jocelyn!"

"It's embarrassing!" she says. She pulls my plate closer to her and takes another bite of my salad.

"Why?" I say. "I mean, how bad can it be?"

"It's pretty bad," she says, sounding pained.

"It can't be as bad as the Blake Letkowski debacle," I say. Blake Letkowski is this kid who I ended up making out with last year when we were working together on a science project. He was bad, bad news. He smoked, he drank, he made racist comments . . . but I loved kissing him. Whoever Jocelyn hooked up with cannot be as bad as Blake Letkowski.

Silence. "Jocelyn?"

"Yeah?"

"Is it?" I pull my math book out of the messenger bag by my feet, hoping feigning nonchalance will get her to spill.

"Is it what?" she asks, frowning.

"Is it better than the Blake Letkowski debacle?"

"Yes. Definitely better."

"Better meaning more of a scandal, or better meaning it isn't as bad?" I say.

"I guess that depends on how you look at it," Jocelyn says slowly. She takes a sip of her chocolate milk. Jocelyn always drinks chocolate milk at lunch. Special, low-carb chocolate milk in single-serving containers that she buys before school each morning at the Mobil on the corner.

"What do you mean?" I say. You'd think I'd be getting bored of this conversation, since she's so obviously jerking me around, but surprisingly, I'm not. I want to know who she hooked up with.

"I mean, do you think it's good that I've hooked up with someone worse than Blake Letkowski, or are you going to be sympathetic?"

"So whoever it is, IS worse than Blake."

"Courtney!"

"WHAT?"

She takes a deep breath. "Never mind, I'm not telling you."

"Fine." I pretend to be engrossed in my math problem. After a few seconds, I can tell she's getting antsy, but I break first. "Just tell me!"

"No!"

"I'll find out."

"No one will find out."

"Why not?"

"Because I'm not going to tell anyone."

"What if *he* tells someone?"

"He won't."

"Why not?"

"Because we both said we wouldn't tell anyone."

"Oh, okay, cause that always works out. Guys who say they won't tell anyone you hooked up always keep their mouths shut." She's silent. "But whatever," I say, shrugging and turning back to my math book. "If you don't want to tell your best friend in the whole world who you hooked up with, well, then . . ." I trail off.

"It's not that I don't want to tell you," she says. "It's just that I don't want to be judged."

"When have I ever judged you?" I say, rolling my eyes. "I am the least judgmental person ever."

"Well," she says, looking thoughtful. She takes another bite of salad. "When I joined newspaper last year because Dan Carlio was on the paper, you kind of judged me."

"That was different," I say. "He was brainwashing you." At the end of junior year, Jocelyn got wrapped up in this ridiculous guy who was one of those activist, literary types. He was always trying to use the school newspaper to further his political beliefs. Jocelyn started skipping school to go to environmental protests and almost lost her credits because of all the time she missed. Plus Dan was really creepy, and he referred to Jocelyn as his "little soldier." Weird.

"He was not!" Jocelyn says. She's horrified.

"Jocelyn, he made you join the Green Party."

"So?"

"So, do you even know what the Green Party is?"

"It has to do with Ralph Nader," she says, proud of herself.

"Whatever."

Silence.

"So tell me."

"Okay."

"Waiting."

"You can't laugh."

"I won't."

"You can't say anything."

"I *won't*."

"B. J. Cartwright."

Silence.

"Say something!" she shrieks.

"You told me not to!" I say. "So I wasn't." B. J. Cartwright. Yikes. That's . . . "disturbing" is really the only word I can come up with, but I can't tell Jocelyn that. Because I told her I wouldn't judge. Besides, Jocelyn takes attacks on people she's hooking up with as a personal attack on herself. So if I were to say to her, "Wow, Jocelyn, that's disturbing," she would take it as meaning, "Wow, Jocelyn, you are disturbed." Which may or may not be true, but still.

"Well, by not saying anything, you're saying a lot."

I think carefully. "Well," I say slowly. "Why don't you tell me how it happened?"

"Okay," she says eagerly. She pushes the empty salad plate away from her. "Well, you know how I was trying to flirt with Mark, right?"

"Right."

"Well, B. J. was hanging out sort of near him, and we started talking."

I try to figure out how I can ask her if this was before or after B. J. clamped onto my leg like some kind of dog in heat, without actually saying, "Hey, Jocelyn, was this before or after B. J. clamped onto my leg like some kind of dog in heat?"

"So we started talking, and then later he called me and invited me to go to Jeremy's party, and then . . . I don't know, really. We ended up back at his house." She stops. "Making out," she adds, in case I missed it.

"Okay," I say slowly. "So what now?"

"Duh," she says. "Now I avoid him."

"Good plan." Pause. "Why, again?"

"Because, hello, it's B. J. Cartwright! Although," she says thoughtfully, "he was a really good kisser."

Ewww.

The bell rings, signaling the end of lunch, and we throw our trays away and head down the hall, me to AP Bio, her to Creative Writing.

"Now," she says, as we stop at her locker on the way. "We're clear on this whole Jordan thing, right?" She twirls the dial to the right.

"What do you mean?" I ask.

"Don't try to talk to him or anything like that," she says. "Ignore him. He's bad news, Courtney."

"Totally," I say. "But what if he says hi to me first?"

"No," she says. "Well, if he says hi first, you can say hi to him. But that's all." She grabs me by the shoulders and looks me straight in the eye, like I'm going off to do battle. "Clear?"

"Totally clear."

before jordan

123 Days Before the Trip, 2:18 p.m.

Courtney McSweeney is acting like I don't exist. We're sitting in math class, and I'm watching her text on her phone through her pink Abercrombie hoodie, and I'm starting to get a little annoyed. Not one word. She hasn't even looked at me.

I raise my hand while Mrs. Novak is going over the homework.

"Yes, Jordan?" she asks.

"I had a question on number nineteen," I say, which isn't true. I don't even know what number nineteen is, but whatever. Mrs. Novak doesn't know that, and hopefully it will get Courtney to look at me. But she doesn't. She just keeps texting. I realize I'm really, really annoyed, which is weird. I don't get annoyed when girls blow me off, especially if I have no interest in them.

"What's your question, Jordan?" Mrs. Novak asks,

looking at me suspiciously. I usually don't raise my hand in math. I usually don't raise my hand in any class. It's not that I don't know the answers. I just find it unnecessary.

"Can we go over the whole problem?" I ask. "Courtney and I were actually discussing how this assignment was a little tricky."

"Sure," Mrs. Novak says, and starts going over the problem. Courtney keeps texting, still not looking at me. What the hell is her problem? Actually, what the hell is *my* problem?

I even made sure I came into the classroom right as the bell was ringing, just in case she had any ideas about us talking. One time sophomore year, I hooked up with this girl (a freshman, figures) who was in five of my classes. It was a nightmare. Every time I'd walk into class, she'd be sitting at my desk, waiting for me, so we could "chat" before the bell rang. That's what she called it — "chatting."

"I just want to chat," she'd say, only her idea of "chatting" involved her asking me ridiculous questions like "Don't you ever get bored with shoes? Since you're a guy and you don't have many choices?"

I learned that if you're in a class with a girl you don't want to talk to, you sneak in just as the bell rings. That way, you avoid having to interact with her. But Courtney hasn't even looked at me. Not once. Even when I mentioned her name.

So when the bell rings signaling the end of the period

and the end of the school day, I wait until she walks out of the classroom, and then walk up behind her, pulling on her hood.

"Hey," I say, when she turns around.

"Oh," she says, looking surprised. "Hey." She shifts her bag to her other shoulder. "What's up?"

"Not much," I say, trying to keep it light. "So is this how you usually treat guys who buy you a meal?"

She smiles. "What do you mean?"

"By ignoring them." I smile back, to show her I'm not bothered by it.

"I wasn't ignoring you," she says, holding up her phone. "I was busy texting."

"Well, I wouldn't want to interrupt whatever secret business it is you were working on."

We've reached her locker now, and she starts to turn the combination dial. She's biting her lip while she does it, and I suddenly have the urge to reach over and bite it for her. Her lip. Not her locker. God, I'm losing it.

"So," she says, sliding some books into her bag. When she does that, it reminds me that the school day is over, and that I might actually have to go home now. Which sends me into a mild panic. After I left Courtney's house on Saturday night, I drove around for a while (okay, a long while), and by the time I got home, it was four in the morning, the rogue car was gone, and my mom was asleep. I slept until around seven (well, tossed around in my bed), and then grabbed breakfast at Dunkin' Donuts and started driving. And driving. And driving. I drove until eleven, called B. J., and spent the day at his house, helping him nurse his hangover and playing Xbox. I ended up crashing at his house, and this morning stopped at my house only when I knew my mom had already gone to work to take a quick shower and change my clothes.

The day, so far, has been a normal Monday at school, but I'm shot. I feel exhausted, but for once, I'm not looking forward to getting home and taking my Monday afternoon nap. I don't want to go home. Now. Or ever. The other thing I realize is that I want to hang out with Courtney. Right now.

"Hey," I say, leaning against her locker and giving her my most charming smile. "What are you doing now?"

"Going home," she says, sliding her backpack over her shoulders and slamming her locker door.

"You want to hang out for a little while, get something to eat or something?"

A look of surprise crosses her face, and she frowns. "I can't," she says firmly. She turns on her heel and starts walking away from me. Which, of course, just makes me want to chase after her. I grab her backpack and pull her around.

"Why not?" I grin.

"Why?" she says.

"No," I say, sighing. "Why not?" What is it with this girl?

"I mean, why do you want to go get something to eat with me?" She puts her hand on her hip, like she's challenging me. She's wearing a small silver chain bracelet and it slides down her wrist.

"Because I'm hungry?" I say. Obviously the best answer isn't "Because I caught my mom having an affair and I don't want to go home." Besides, it's not like I'm lying. I am hungry. And I do want to hang out with her. Plus, why is she challenging me? Who says shit like this?

She turns and starts walking away again. "Courtney!" I'm literally chasing her now, making my way down the hall and through the throng of people leaving for the day.

"Yeah?" She turns around.

"What is your problem? If you don't want to go, just say it."

"I don't want to go." She crosses her arms in front of her.

"Fine," I say. "Then that's all you had to say." I turn on my heel and start walking down the hall.

"Jordan!" she calls after me, and I almost don't stop. But she says my name again, and I turn around.

"Look," she says, "I'm sorry. It's just been a weird day, that's all." She bites her lip. "If you still want to go . . ."

"Don't feel like you have to do me any favors," I say, still a little pissed. "It's not a big deal. If you don't want to go, you don't want to go."

"No," she says, pushing her hair away from her face. "I do want to go. But I'm buying."

"Fine," I say, shrugging. "Then let's go."

* * *

Half an hour later, we're sitting in my truck, eating drive-thru food from Taco Bell. I wanted to go to a real place, but she was adamant that we go for fast food. This chick is really strange, because then she wouldn't even let me take her INTO the restaurant, and instead insisted on eating in my car.

"So," I say, "thanks for ignoring me today."

"I wasn't ignoring you," she says, looking uncomfortable. She shifts in her seat. "I was just paying attention."

"Right," I say. I take a bite of my Taco Supreme and look over at her. She's barely touched her food. Plus, she keeps giving me all these one-word answers. I grope for something to say that will force her to engage in conversation with me.

"So," I say. "Tell me about your parents."

"My parents?" she asks.

"Yeah. Why you don't have the same last name as them, if and how they're involved in the whole drug trafficking scheme, any neuroses they may have, if you hate them, etc."

"It's really not that scandalous," she says. "So if I tell you, it may ruin the whole thing. Maybe I should keep it a secret, so you'll think I'm mysterious and engaging."

"I already think you're mysterious and engaging," I say, taking a sip of my soda.

"You do?" She turns to me, and the sun shining through my windshield hits her hair and illuminates her face. She smiles. "Why?"

"Why what?" I say. Suddenly I feel weird. For the first

time, I realize I'm in a car with a girl. Not only that, but it's just hit me that Courtney's fucking hot. Not hot in the way Madison is, with her revealing clothes and huge amounts of lipstick, but hot in the sense of . . . I don't know. Just hot. An overall package of hotness.

"Why am I mysterious and engaging?" she asks, sounding exasperated.

"Oh," I say. "Because you ignored me in math today. And no one ever ignores me."

She rolls her eyes. "Right. No one ever ignores you."

"Well," I say, looking at her out of the corner of my eye. "Sometimes girls do ignore me. But it's only because they want me to think they're ignoring me, so that I'll want them."

"Maybe they're ignoring you because they don't want you." She shrugs. "Maybe they're just weirded out by the fact that you've basically ignored them for four years of high school, and then started randomly taking them to drive-thrus and diners at weird times."

"Except I don't usually take girls to random drive-thrus and diners at weird times."

"Where do you usually take them?" She's smiling at me now, and I smile back.

"The backseat," I joke, and the smile vanishes from her face. "Whoa," I say, "just kidding." This girl is such a hardass. "Lighten up, Court."

She takes a small bite of her taco and stares out the window.

"So," I say. "Your parents? What's the deal?"

"My dad isn't my biological father," she says, shrugging. "He adopted me last year, but I just decided to keep my last name. Didn't want to have to go through the hassle of changing it, but I might at some point."

"That's cool," I say, hoping she doesn't ask about my parents and what the deal is with them. No way we need to get into the fact that my mom is screwing around on my dad. "Is your dad a good guy?"

"Yeah," she says. "He's great. He's been married to my mom since I was three, so I don't really know anything else, you know?"

"Cool." I take the last bite of my taco and throw the balled-up wrapper back into the empty bag. "So what should we do now, Court?"

"Why do you keep calling me 'Court'?" she asks.

"Because," I say, shrugging. "It's my new pet name for you."

"As opposed to your old pet name?"

"Yeah, my old pet name," I say, miming that I'm texting someone on a phone. "'Weird Text Girl.'" It's a gamble, but it pays off. She reaches over and pushes me playfully, and I block her hand. I realize again how good she smells, and I swallow. No way I'm going to start hooking up with Courtney McSweeney. That's just insane.

"Are you flirting with me?" I ask.

"No." She looks shocked and moves back to her side of the car. "Not even."

"You totally were."

"Sweetie," she says, turning to look at me. "If I was flirting with you, you'd know it."

She raises her eyebrows at me, and I realize she's probably telling the truth. If she were flirting with me, I'd probably know it. I'm also really, really turned on.

An hour later, we're in the DVD section at Barnes & Noble, debating whether or not *Laguna Beach* is a good TV show. I somehow conned her into coming into the bookstore with me, which wasn't that hard since it's right next door to Taco Bell.

"They're like talking mannequins," Courtney says, shaking her head. "I have no idea how you could remotely be interested in this show."

"I didn't say I was interested in it," I say, rolling my eyes. This is a lie. I watch it all the time.

"What night of the week is it on?" she asks, raising her eyebrows.

"Wednesday," I recite without thinking. She smiles smugly.

"That doesn't mean anything!" I protest. She slides the DVD of *Laguna* back onto the shelf and turns around.

"Whatever." She shrugs and starts walking toward the Action/Adventure movies.

"Everyone knows *Laguna Beach* is on Wednesday nights! All you have to do is turn on MTV for half a second. There's commercials on all the time."

"Fine," she says again, shrugging.

"And so what if I watch it?" I say, "It is what it is."

"*Ridiculous* is what it is. They're like pod people."

"Okay," I say, switching tactics. "Did you watch *The OC*?"

"Totally different," she says.

"Oh my God, not even!" I say. "It's the same thing. Only one is written for television, and one is reality TV."

"*The OC* is completely different," she says. "Because even though the characters are rich and materialistic, they at least have intelligent conversations. They have issues. Dilemmas. Debates!"

Hmm. She has a point. I'm trying to think of a good *Laguna* debate that didn't involve the Kristin Cavallari/Nick Lachey situation in the media. My cell phone rings before I can think of one, and I pull it out of my pocket.

It's B. J. I hesitate. It's probably rude to answer it, but Courtney's not going to want to hang out with me forever, so it's a good bet that at some point, I'm going to need to head over to B. J.'s to avoid going home. In which case answering the phone is going to be in my best interest.

"Do you mind if I take this?" I ask. "It's kind of important."

"No problem," she says, turning back to the movies. She kneels down to get a look at something on the bottom shelf, and the back of her shirt rises up, showing her back. I swallow.

"Whaddup?" I say, flipping my phone open and walking a few feet away from Courtney.

"Dude, shit is going down," B. J. says, sounding like shit really is going down.

"What is it?"

"So I just got out of the gym, right?" B. J. stays after with the football team every day to work out, so I'm assuming that's what he's referring to.

"Yeah," I say.

"So when I leave the school, there's Jocelyn, in the parking lot with Krista Crause and Tia Biddlecome."

"Okay," I say, already starting to become bored with this story. I'm a little bitter about B. J.'s whole hookup with Jocelyn, since after I got him coffee the other night and drove him home, he ended up going to Jeremy's party anyway. So while I was catching my mom cheating on my dad and acting insane about Courtney McSweeney, B. J. was out partying without me. I try to catch a glimpse of Courtney's bare back again by glancing around the display of *Star Wars* DVDs. She's still leaning. She has a nice ass. I wonder what kind of underwear she wears, if it's a thong, or maybe those boy shorts. Something lacy, maybe.

"And she ignores me!" B. J. says. Courtney leans over farther. Her shirt slides farther up her back. I try to figure out how close I need to be to get the best view without her actually hearing my conversation. Is it insane to be having these thoughts about her? Probably. I mean, I'm supposed to be kicking it to Madison. It's just that Courtney's fun to be around. She takes my mind off all the shit that's going on at home. Which is good.

"Hello?!" B. J. asks on the other end of the phone.

"Yeah," I say, swallowing. "Jocelyn ignored you."

"I can't believe it!" he says. "That's fucked up, dude."

"Girls are fucked up," I say, shrugging. "Do you like her?"

"Not anymore," he says, not sounding like he means it. "Not if she's going to act like a shit."

"She's messing with you," I say. "Just ignore her right back."

"But I don't want to fucking ignore her," B. J. says. "I want to hook up with her again!"

"I know," I say, sighing. "But if she's going to play it all cool, the last thing you want is to come off as Psycho Obsessed Asshole."

A Barnes & Noble employee, a young guy in a green apron with pierced ears almost bumps into me. "Sorry," I say.

"Where are you?" B. J. asks suspiciously.

"At the bookstore."

"The bookstore? What the fuck for?"

"I'm, uh, looking at books," I say. "And I should get back to it. Let me call you later."

"Who are you with?" B. J. asks.

Fuck. "What do you mean?" I ask, trying to infuse my voice with as much innocence as possible. He sighs.

"Who. Are. You. There. With."

"I'm by myself," I lie. Why did I just lie? I hate lying. I

don't believe in lying. Lying only gets you in trouble. Manipulating situations is one thing, but lying is another. My theory (especially with girls), is that if you don't lie, you can't be held responsible for anything bad that goes down.

Case in point: When I hooked up with Jana Freeze last summer. I told her I didn't want a girlfriend, and that I was going to be hooking up with other people. She got all pissed off when I kissed Michelle Tessiro the weekend after. But really, it wasn't my fault. Because she knew the deal, and she chose to put herself in that situation.

I know I sound like a slut. But I'm really not.

"You're by yourself?" B. J. asks incredulously. "What the fuck for?"

"I told you," I say, trying not to lose my patience, since it's really my fault for lying to him. "I'm looking at books."

"Dude, that's some fucked-up shit," he says.

"Fine," I say. "I'm with Courtney McSweeney."

"Courtney McSweeney?" B. J. asks, as if I've just announced I'm out on a date with Mischa Barton. "What the fuck for?"

"I don't know," I say, realizing it's true.

"Whatever," B. J. says. "Can you maybe ask her about Jocelyn for me?"

"Ask her what about Jocelyn?"

"Ask her what the deal is. They're friends." He sighs as if he can't believe my obvious ridiculousness at not getting the plan. Which is really worrisome to me, because if B. J. is saying something I'm not understanding, that means my head is completely fucked up.

"Okay," I agree.

"But don't let her know I want to know," he instructs.

"Of course not." I don't point out that expecting me to ask a girl I hardly know about how her friend feels about B. J. without actually telling her why I want to know is going to be a pretty hard thing to do.

"Lata." B. J. clicks off before I can make plans with him for later. Shit.

Courtney comes around the corner, carrying *Laguna Beach* Season One on DVD. She holds it up and smiles at me. "Maybe I'll give it a second chance."

"You should," I say, grabbing the blue DVD case out of her hand and checking out the back. What's not to like about this show? Hot girls. Hookups. Who needs intelligent conversations and debates? It all boils down to wanting one another, anyway. So people should just hook up and get it over with.

"So . . ." she says, taking it back from me. "I should probably get home."

"Oh," I say, kind of surprised. Girls don't usually end dates with me. Not that this is really a date. It's more like a hang out. I follow her up to the cash register, where she purchases the *Laguna Beach* DVDs. Definitely not a date. Because if it were a date, I'd be paying. And we'd be hooking up. And that is definitely not going to happen.

Half an hour later, we're kissing in my car.

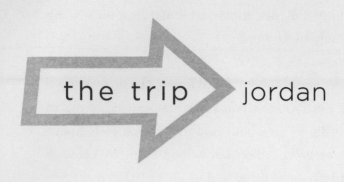

the trip jordan

Day One, 12:36 p.m.

I'm heading toward the bathroom to see what's taking Courtney so long when I see her lean over and throw up all over the floor. It's pretty nasty, a bunch of brown chunks and green liquid. I knew that sausage calzone didn't look right.

"Court," I say, rushing over to her. "Are you okay?"

She looks up at me, her eyes bloodshot, and then leans over and heaves again. I take her cell phone out of her hand, hang up on whoever it is she was talking to without bothering to say anything, and lead Courtney past the line of waiting women (who are all staring—have they never seen anyone upchuck before?) and into the women's bathroom.

"Jordan," she says, leaning against my shoulder. "You can't come into the girls' bathroom."

Four women at the sink are gaping at me openly. "It's okay," I say to them. "I'm just helping my friend. She's not feeling so well."

"We're not friends," Courtney says, and then throws up again into one of the sinks against the wall. It's not the best move, saying the guy who's taking care of you isn't your friend, but I let it slide since she's obviously in distress. I pull her hair back from her face.

"Do you have a hair tie?" I ask her, ignoring the stares of the woman at the sinks. What is their problem? Do they not see that she's sick? You'd think they'd be rallying around me, excited I was so obviously concerned that I would risk a trip into the women's bathroom. Maybe it's a new kind of crime, guys pretending they're friends with random girls who get sick at rest stops, so that they can sneak into women's bathrooms and get a peek at . . . I look around. At middle-aged women washing their hands.

Courtney hands me her bag, and I riffle through it, looking for a hair tie. Makeup, notebook, mirror . . . why do girls need so much stuff? I pull Courtney's hair back from her face, trying to gather it in a ponytail. Her skin feels smooth against my hands.

"Let me do it," Courtney says, taking the hair tie away from me. Her fingers brush against mine, and my heart rate speeds up again. God, I want her so bad.

She pulls her hair back, then leans over the sink again and gives one final, silent heave. I rub her back until her body stops shaking.

"You okay?" I say.

"Yeah," she says. She's gripping the sides of the sink so

hard that her knuckles are turning white. "I'm okay. I just hate throwing up."

"Will you be okay in here for a second by yourself? I'll go get you a bottle of water."

"Okay," she says, not really sounding like she means it. I look around the bathroom. The floors are dirty and there are random paper towels and toilet paper strewn around the floor. It smells like exactly what you'd think a thruway rest stop bathroom would smell like.

"Actually," I say. "Why don't you just come with me? We'll get you some water, and then you can sit in the back of my truck. Some air might make you feel better."

"Okay," she agrees, and starts walking shakily toward the door of the restroom. I go to put my arm around her like before, but she shrugs me off. "I'm fine."

Ten minutes later, she's sitting with her feet hanging over the side of my open truck back, sipping water slowly, and looking a little bit better, although really pale.

"I should call Jocelyn back," she says. "I was talking to her when I started throwing up."

I feel relieved that she wasn't talking to Lloyd, which is completely ridiculous. Courtney and I are over, and no matter how much I still want to be with her, it's not going to happen. And she deserves someone who's going to make her happy. If Lloyd does that for her, I really am cool with it.

My phone starts ringing in my pocket, and I check the

caller ID. Courtney's dad. The fucker will not leave me alone. Every five minutes with him.

"I'm gonna take this," I tell Court. "Are you going to be okay for a few minutes?"

"Yeah," she says. "I'll call Jocelyn back so she doesn't worry."

I walk safely out of Courtney's earshot, and then open my phone. "What?" I say. He may have gotten me to break up with Courtney, but as far as I'm concerned, the power he has over me stops there. Well, that's not exactly true. Because he keeps calling me.

"That's not a nice way to answer the phone, Jordan," he says, sounding cheerful.

"Yeah, well, I'm not in exactly the nicest mood right now," I say.

"Oh, and why's that?" he asks, sounding amused.

"Because you keep calling me."

"I just wanted to make sure everything was going okay," he says. "That the trip was proceeding safely."

"Yeah, everything's fine," I say, not mentioning the fact that Courtney just spent ten minutes throwing up into a sink.

"Jordan, you know I'm not trying to be a dick about this," he says, sighing.

"Yeah, spare me," I say, watching Courtney from where I'm standing. She looks really small and really pale.

"I'm not," Mr. Brewster says. "I just want Courtney to be happy, and I really think this is the best way to go about it. And Jordan, I think you know that telling Courtney what happened really isn't going to serve any real purpose."

Other than to make her hate me, I think to myself. And it's true. If I told Courtney what I knew, she would hate me even more than she does now. And having her hate me because she thinks I dumped her for another girl is much better than having her hate me because of what I know.

"Well, you don't have to worry," I say, swallowing hard. "I'm not going to say anything."

"Thanks," Mr. Brewster says. "I really do appreciate it, Jordan. And I *am* going to tell Courtney. But on my own time."

"Whatever," I say. I snap my phone shut and take a deep breath. After a few seconds, I turn back around and head back to the truck. I cannot wait until this trip is over.

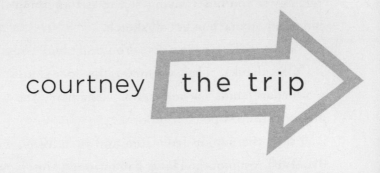

courtney the trip

Day One, 1:47 p.m.

I'm going to throw up again. "I'm going to throw up again," I tell Jordan, feeling it rising up in my throat. We're back on the highway now, and he signals and pulls over quickly to the side of the road. I open the door and lean out, throwing up onto the pavement. This is so disgusting. Seriously. I hate throwing up. I have this really bad phobic fear of it. I go to great lengths not to throw up, and until today, I hadn't thrown up since the fourth grade. Fourth grade! That's like eight years. It's a real phobia, too. Throwing up, I mean. I know no one likes to throw up, but it's proven that some people are really scared of it. Like me. And some celebrities. Matthew McConaughey, I think.

"You okay?" Jordan asks, and I feel his hand on my back.

"Yeah, I'm okay," I lie, wiping my mouth on the back of my hand. Gross, gross, gross. I'll bet his MySpace girl never throws up all over herself when they're together. I'll bet they're too busy having sex to eat anything that might cause her stomach to get all sketch.

"You sure?" Jordan asks. "You don't look okay."

"Gee, thanks," I say, slamming the door shut.

Jordan hands me a napkin. "Uh, here," he says, "you might want to wipe your mouth."

I take the napkin from him and turn away, wiping the drool off my mouth. Have I mentioned this is really disgusting?

I throw the napkin into the ashtray and push the seat back again, reclining all the way back. It's actually very easy to trick yourself into not throwing up. You just lay back, perfectly still and straight, close your eyes, and try not to move.

"Hey, Court?"

"Yes?" I ask, trying not to move my mouth in case it sets off some kind of motion wave to my stomach.

"Listen, I think maybe we should check into a hotel somewhere," he says, sounding hesitant, like he doesn't want to piss me off. "You're obviously sick, and you need to rest."

"I'm fine," I say. "And besides, it would mess up the schedule." Is he crazy? We're already way behind thanks to his lollygagging this morning. Plus the traffic. Plus the long bathroom lines at the rest stop. Plus my throwing up.

"Are you sure?" he says, "Because I saw a sign a few miles back for a Days Inn coming up."

"It. Would. Mess. Up. The. Schedule."

"Okay," he says, looking at me out of the corner of his eye. "Are you sure?"

"YES." Of course I'm sure. I'm not going to let throwing up stop me from getting to college on time.

Two miles later, after we've had to pull over three more times so I can throw up, he pulls off at the next exit and follows the sign that says DAYS INN. I don't stop him.

So this is really awkward. Jordan's checking into the Days Inn, which is a completely and totally unscheduled stop, and the front desk clerk has assumed we want one room. This place is kind of sketch (the clerk asked us for how long we wanted the room, and I think he meant in hours), and there are some very scantily dressed girls standing outside. Which is weird, because it's four in the afternoon. Definitely not late enough for prostitution. Although maybe I've been conditioned by the media to think prostitutes only come out after midnight. Like this one special I saw once about hookers who frequent truckstops. They call them "lot lizards" and they only come out at night.

"Yes," Jordan says. "We'll take the one room."

"No," I say. "We'll take two."

The guy looks nervously between the two of us. "No, we won't," Jordan says, turning out to look at me. I'm sprawled in one of the chairs in the "lobby," which is really a foyer. I have vomit on my shirt, my hair is coming out of my ponytail, and on the way in here, I almost fell over and Jordan had to take my bag. "Court, you're sick. I'm not leaving you by yourself."

"Fine," I say. "But two beds."

"Of course," Jordan says, rolling his eyes.

Of course two beds. I forgot for a moment that Jordan has a girlfriend. One who he obviously loves enough to leave me for, which means there's no way the thought of sharing a bed with me would have crossed his mind. For the first time, I wonder what his girlfriend thinks of the fact that Jordan is here, on a trip with me. She's probably one of those super-secure girls who is all confident in her relationship. How annoying.

Conversations About Me Jordan Had with His Girlfriend (A Deluded Fantasy by Courtney Elizabeth McSweeney):

Jordan: So I'm stuck going on this trip with Courtney.

Mercedes: Okay.

Jordan: Just so you know, nothing's going to happen.

Mercedes (starts taking her clothes off so she and Jordan can have sex): I know.

Jordan: You want to have sex again? We just finished two hours ago.

Mercedes (climbs on top of him): Yes. **(Pauses.)** This Courtney girl or whatever her name is, she's not cute, is she?

Jordan: No.

Mercedes: Cool.

Jordan picks up our bags and starts down the hall. "Room 103," he says, reading off the card the front desk guy gave him. I'm concentrating on making it down the hall without passing out, since the floor seems to be spinning. I'm watching my feet (which are cased in very cute purple sandals) as I move one in front of the other, trying not to lose it. One. Two. Step. Step. Ha, like that song by Ciara. "I love it when you one, two step." Although I don't think Ciara was trying to keep herself upright while walking down a hotel room hallway with her ex-boyfriend who she was still in love with when she wrote that song. I think Ciara was having dance parties and fun and all sorts of really good things that had nothing to do with nausea or horrible road trips.

I lean against the door frame as Jordan slides the plastic card into the electronic sensor that will let us into our room. A green light flashes and he holds the door open for me. I push by him, and as I do, my chest brushes against his, and for a second, I lose my breath, but then I'm past him and it's over. I slide onto one of the beds and drop my bag onto the floor.

Whoever was in the room before left the air conditioner on full-blast, and it feels good. I'm hot. I lean back on the bed and close my eyes.

"You okay?" Jordan asks, plopping himself down on the other bed.

"Yeah," I say. "I'm fine."

He picks the remote off the floor and turns on the TV. The sounds of ESPN come blaring out of the speakers.

I pick my suitcase up off the floor and head to the bathroom without telling him where I'm going. I take a long, cool shower, then change into a pair of soft pink pajama shorts and a black spaghetti-strapped tank top. I feel much better. I pull my cell out of my purse. Three missed calls. My dad. Jocelyn. And Lloyd.

Shit. Lloyd. I almost forgot about him.

Whatever, I'm not going to think about that now. La, la, la. Just going to call Jocelyn back. I dial her cell number.

"Hey," I say when she answers. "Did you call?"

"Yeah," she says. "I wanted to see how you were feeling."

I hear the sound of car horns honking in the background.

"Uh, Joce?" I ask. "What are you doing?"

"I'm tailing B. J. to McDonald's," she says, sounding satisfied.

"Tailing B. J. to McDonald's?" I repeat dumbly. She can't be serious. Who does that outside of Veronica Mars?

"Yeah," she says. "I'm following him to see if he goes to Katelyn's."

"Who?"

"Katelyn Masters. Who he hooked up with freshman year?"

"Why would he be going to see Katelyn Masters?" I ask, confused.

"Because she left him a MySpace message that was semi-flirty, and then today he was very vague about what he was doing. So I headed over to his house and waited outside until he left. And now he's at McDonald's, and I'm following him to see where else he's going." MySpace is seriously going to be responsible for everyone losing their minds.

"Aren't you afraid he's going to see you?"

"No, not at all," she says. "I'm staying far enough behind him, and besides, I'm in my mom's car."

"Why are you in your mom's car?" Jocelyn has a perfectly good car, a black Honda Civic, which her parents bought her a few months ago as an early graduation present.

"Duh," she says. "Because I don't want him to figure out I'm following him."

"Hey, Joce?" I say, trying to sound gentle. "Wouldn't it be easier just to ask him where exactly he's going?"

"Courtney," she says, sighing in exasperation. "I can't ask him! He'll think I don't trust him."

"You obviously don't."

"Asshole!" Jocelyn screams. "Sorry, some guy tried to cut me off while turning in to Home Depot. What were you saying?"

"I don't remember," I say, scared by Jocelyn's sudden road rage.

"Oh, right, about B. J. and me. How I don't trust him."

"Why would you want to be with someone you don't trust?"

"I wouldn't. But what if I confront him on it and it turns out not to be true, and he breaks up with me because he thinks I don't trust him?"

"But you don't!"

"True." She considers this. "But it could be all my own psychosis."

"Probably."

More car horns honking. "I gotta go—I think B. J.'s coming out of the drive-thru, and I don't want to lose him."

"I'll call ya later," I say, clicking off.

I look at the phone and consider calling Lloyd, but then I slide it back into my bag. I'll deal with it later.

When I get back to the room, Jordan's sitting on the bed, flipping between a poker tournament and a baseball game.

"Hey," he says. "You okay?"

"Yeah," I tell him. "I'm fine." The truth is, I don't know if I'm fine or not. Suddenly, I feel totally exhausted, like I can't even move. I haul myself up onto the second bed, pull the covers down, and grab one of the pillows from the top of the bed. I move it to the bottom. I like to sleep upside down on beds. Plus, the way the room is set up, the TV is closer to the bottom of the bed, so it makes sense. Not that I care about watching poker. But I wouldn't mind watching the baseball game.

"Who's playing?" I ask Jordan. My eyes feel really heavy, and my throat feels scratchy from throwing up so much.

"The Devil Rays and the Yankees," he says softly, looking at me. I meet his eye for a second, and then look away. Jordan and I spent almost every night this summer watching the Devil Rays on TV. And on one of our very first dates, we went to a game. Whatever. Not thinking about it. "Do you want to watch something else?" he asks.

"No," I say, my eyes closing. "I'm really, really tired."

"Yeah," he says. "You should probably get some rest."

"Probably," I say. I must have fallen asleep in about two minutes, because the next thing I know, I open my eyes, and the clock says it's four in the morning. Which means I've slept for like fifteen hours. My stomach feels hollow and tired, like it's been through an ordeal. Which I guess it has. I let my eyes adjust to the darkness of the room. And then I realize Jordan's next to me, sleeping, his arms wrapped around me, our legs tangled together under the blanket.

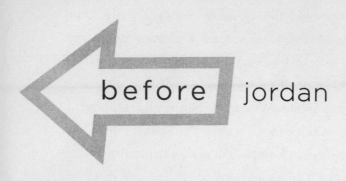

before jordan

123 Days Before the Trip, 4:30 p.m.

I'm trying to kiss Courtney McSweeney. If you had asked me six months ago if I would ever be making out with Courtney McSweeney, I would have said no, absofuckinglutely not. But here I am, trying to get her to kiss me. We're parked in front of her house, sitting in my car, and somehow I pulled her close to me before she could get out of the car. Which she let me do. But then, when I went to kiss her, she turned her head.

"Not gonna happen," she says, her voice muffled against my chest.

"Why not?" I ask, wondering if I've underestimated her. Maybe she's a game player, one of those girls who makes you work for it. The weird thing is, I'm usually into that, but thinking about Courtney messing with my head is disappointing for some reason.

"Because," she says. "Once you cross that line with someone, you can never take it back."

"What do you mean?" I ask. Why would she want to take it back? I'm a very good kisser. Or so I've been told.

"I mean that once you kiss someone, all this other stuff comes into it, whether you want it to or not."

"Not necessarily," I say. I'm stroking her hair now, and all she would have to do is move her face about two inches and tilt it up, and we'd be kissing.

"It does," she says. "It brings all kinds of drama you never have to deal with if you just stay friends."

"Not true." I try to pull her closer, which doesn't really work, because she's already as close as she's going to get. "I've had hookups that haven't resulted in any kind of drama."

"None whatsoever?"

"Nope."

"No broken hearts?"

"Nope."

"No psychotic prank phone calls?"

"Nope."

"No feeling like you wanted to throw up and/or kill her new boyfriend?"

"Nope."

"Name one girl you hooked up with that you're still friends with."

"Nope."

"That's what I thought," she says smugly. Although being smug really makes no sense here, because I think she really does want to kiss me. Otherwise why would she be leaning against me like that?

"You tricked me," I say.

"So do it, then. Name one girl you hooked up with that you're still friends with."

"It doesn't have to be dramatic," I say, ignoring her request. "It can just be about . . . the moment."

"I'm not good with the moment," she says. "I'm always worried about what's going to happen next."

"You should stop worrying," I say. And then I reach down and tilt her face up toward mine, and I kiss her. She doesn't pull away. Her mouth is on mine, and our tongues are together, and my hands are on her face. And it's really, really nice. She pulls away first, and we lean our heads together.

"That was nice," I say, smiling.

"That was such a mistake," she says, smiling back. And then she gets out of my car and heads into her house without looking back.

When I get to my house fifteen minutes later, my mom is sitting at the kitchen table. So much for waiting it out and hiding until I got up the courage to confront her. She's wearing a purple sweater set and a cream-colored skirt. Which is weird. Because she looks . . . normal. Not like she was just fucking some random dude on the couch that her and my dad picked out for their anniversary.

"Jordan," she says, standing up and smoothing down

her skirt. Her eyes glance at me nervously and I look away. "Listen, we should talk."

"I don't know if we have anything to talk about," I say simply. I'm trying to figure out the best way to work this to my advantage. I'm pissed.

"We have to," she says. "Sit down."

I pull out a chair from the kitchen table and plop down across from her.

"What do you want to talk about?" I look at her, and suddenly, I'm really, really scared. It's something on her face. Because here's the thing—up until this point, I figured it was just a random thing. Maybe her and a client were working late and got carried away. They started kissing, I came in, and she sent him home after she came to her senses. That's how these things usually work, don't they? I curse myself for watching *Laguna Beach* instead of learning valuable life lessons on *The OC*.

"I think we need to talk about what went on here the other night." She bites her lip again and looks around nervously.

"What about it?"

"Jordan, I really, really, need for you not to tell your father about what happened until I have a chance to talk with him."

"You can't be serious," I say. "There's no way I'm not going to tell Dad about this." She must be delusional. Does she really think I would keep this kind of huge secret from my dad? How can she even expect me to do that?

"Jordan," she says, "I have the right to be able to tell him on my own time, on my own grounds." She tugs on the hem of her skirt nervously. "That's the only way we're going to be able to work it out."

"Whatever," I say, heading to the refrigerator and grabbing a Coke out of the side door. "I'm staying out of it. In fact, I'm totally over it."

I leave her standing in the kitchen and head up to my room, where I spend the next two hours listening to rap music on my iPod and thinking about how it felt to kiss Courtney McSweeney.

courtney the trip

Day Two, 4:07 a.m.

I lay there for a second, not really sure what I'm supposed to do. I mean, Jordan is in the same bed with me. Wrapped around me. A part of me wants to scream, to push him off, to flip out, and possibly kick him in the balls. But it feels good. To be close to him. And I realize that I'm probably never going to be this close to him again. Ever. So maybe I should just give into it for a little while, hold on to this last thing.

I can feel his chest moving next to me, up and down with his breathing, and his arms feel strong around me. My stomach grumbles, probably because it's empty. What a pain in the ass. I know I can't eat anything, because if I do, I'm going to end up sick again.

I push Jordan's hand off my shoulder. It bumps my head. Great. Why is he in this bed with me? Is it possible I got into some kind of weird delusional state because of my apparent food poisoning and then grabbed him and pulled him into bed with me? Maybe it was a fugue. We learned about those in psych class. I'm horrified.

I push his arm up and over my head, trying not to wake him up. The last thing I want is for him to be aware of the fact that we're in this position. Maybe it happened naturally. Like in movies, when guys and girls are always falling asleep and not realizing they're getting wrapped around each other. Maybe it's our bodies' way of telling us we were meant to be. Or maybe I, like, cuddle raped him or something.

I need to get out of this bed. Out of this hotel. Out of this trip. It's definitely not good for my mental state. I grab my phone off the nightstand by the bed, extract myself quickly from the tangle that is Jordan, and head to the bathroom. I check my missed calls. Four of them. They're all Lloyd. Lovely.

I wonder if four in the morning is too late/early to call him. Actually, it could be the perfect time, because there's no way he's going to be awake. So I can leave him a quick message, a "Thanks for calling me, but I was sick and sleeping," kind of message, so that I won't actually have to talk to him. I'm so brilliant.

I push the button in my phone book next to his name and listen while it rings. Ring . . . Ring . . .

"Hello?" he says, sounding tired.

Great. What kind of fool answers their phone at four in the morning? On the day they get to school, nonetheless!

Doesn't he have orientation? Whatever. This is so ridiculous. I mean, I hooked up with him, it's not the end of the world. People hook up all the time. And then you just deal with it. You talk about it. You work it out. This is Lloyd. He's my friend. He's not psychotic. He's Lloyd. I take a deep breath.

"Oh, hi," I say.

"I miss you."

"Oh." It's the only thing I can think of to say. I don't have to say it back, right? I mean, it's not like when someone says "I love you," and you're kind of obligated to say it back, even if you don't mean it. And I do miss him. Kind of. Although I don't really know how you can miss someone you just saw one night ago. I mean, normally, we don't see each other every day. So it's kind of weird for him to say he's missing me, since even though we're both going to be away at school, nothing's really changed yet.

"What time is it?" I hear the sound of him moving around in his bed.

"Um, four in the morning," I say.

"I'm so glad you called me back," he says. "I was worried about you."

"Yeah," I say. Silence. "So, listen, I can't really talk for that long, because I'm in the bathroom and I don't want to wake Jordan up."

"Why would you wake Jordan up?" he asks, sounding confused.

"Because he might hear me talking, and then he would wake up. And having to deal with him while he's awake during normal hours is enough of a trial for me." I'm assuming Lloyd will like the fact that I'm saying something bad about Jordan, but my statement has the opposite effect. Lloyd flips out.

"You guys are staying in the same room?" he asks. Suddenly he sounds wide awake, and there's more noise on the other end of the line, like he's sitting up and taking notice. Suddenly, I feel like I'm in some really weird episode of *The Twilight Zone*, where Lloyd wants me and I don't want him, Jordan broke up with me, I'm in bad hotel room lighting, and it's four in the morning. But it's not. It's real life. So weird.

"Yeah, we're staying in the same room," I say, trying to sound breezy. "But there's two beds, and it was only because there was only one room left." I'm now lying to Lloyd. I'm a liar.

"There was only one room?" Lloyd asks incredulously. Apparently a very bad liar.

"Yup," I say.

"I'm sorry, Court," he says. "Are you okay? Having to stay in the same room with him like that?"

"Yeah, it's fine," I say. "I'm holding up."

"Good."

"Yup," I say. "So, anyway, you sound really tired, so I should let you go. I'll call you tomorrow, though, before we get there and let you know when—"

"Today," Lloyd says.

"Today what?" I ask. My head is starting to hurt, and I'm not sure if it's because I'm getting over some sort of whacked-out food poisoning thing, or if it's because of the stress of this trip.

"You'll be here today, technically," Lloyd says. "Because it's four in the morning?"

"Oh," I say. "Right." Silence.

"Are you sure everything's okay?" Lloyd asks.

"Yeah," I say. "It's fine."

"Is it Jordan? Has he tried anything?"

"Uh, no," I say. "He hasn't. Tried anything, I mean. He has a girlfriend." I don't mention the fact that I just woke up with Jordan's arms wrapped around me. Because that was obviously some sort of weird mistake, something that happened while we were sleeping.

"Like that's going to stop him." Lloyd snorts. No, really, he snorts. The guy I made out with last night is snorting. "You guys were together when he started hooking up with his new girlfriend, so I wouldn't put anything past him, Courtney."

I want to point out that (allegedly) Jordan didn't cheat on me, but really, what's the point? Lloyd is going to believe what he believes. And whatever, he's probably right. Jordan probably did cheat on me. I feel myself starting to get upset, and I take a deep breath.

"Okay, well, I'm going to go back to sleep," I say to

Lloyd. "I'll give you a call tomorrow and let you know how we're progressing."

"Okay," Lloyd says. "I miss you, Courtney, and I can't wait to see you."

"Yeah, you too," I say, and then hang up before he can say anything else. I slide my cell phone back into my bag and creep back into the room. I climb into the other bed, the one Jordan's not in, close my eyes, and try to fall asleep.

courtney ← before

107 Days Before the Trip, 4:05 p.m.

"Stop hooking up with him," Jocelyn says. "It's going to get bad."

"What do you mean?" I ask, frowning.

"Just what I said. You like him, Court. And that's not good."

"I don't like him," I say, rolling my eyes. "We're just, you know, hanging out." It's been a couple of weeks since I first kissed Jordan, and after a couple of days of me trying to blow him off, and him being very persistent, we've been hanging out a lot lately. And by a lot, I mean, um, a lot. As in, like, every second that we're not at school, we're together. And even when we're in school, we're texting. Or hanging out at lunch or during our unstructureds in the library. Or passing notes in math. It's really not that bad, though. I mean, school is almost over. So it's not like we have a ton of work we should be concentrating on or anything.

"You like him," Jocelyn says. "I can tell from the way you talk to him. And it's not good. When people start liking people, that's when someone has the ability to get hurt."

"I'm not going to get hurt," I say, shrugging. We're sitting in Jocelyn's living room, watching my DVD set of *Laguna Beach* and talking about nothing.

"Just be careful, that's all I'm saying."

"You should talk," I say, picking up a pillow from my side of the couch and throwing it at her.

"Totally different," she says. "I'm not nearly as emotionally attached to B. J. as you are to Jordan."

"I'm not emotionally attached to Jordan," I lie. The truth is, I kind of am. Emotionally attached to him, I mean. At first, it was just fun. I liked kissing him, and being around him, and holding his hand. But then it turned into something different. I talk to him. I tell him things I've never really told anyone, like about how I'm afraid once I get to college everything will be different, and I won't be smart anymore, and I'll end up flunking out and my parents will disown me.

"Well, whatever," Jocelyn says. She grabs the remote and turns up the volume on the TV. "Just be careful, Courtney. Because he is most definitely not emotionally attached to you."

jordan ⬅ before

99 Days Before the Trip, 6:07 p.m.

I think I'm emotionally attached to Courtney McSweeney. This is not a good plan for a few reasons. I make it a point to never get emotionally attached to anyone. Emotional attachments are messy. They end with broken hearts and stalking. Not that I've ever been on that end of it, i.e., been the one who was stalking or getting brokenhearted. But I've seen plenty of girls get emotionally attached to me, and it's never a good situation. Emotional attachments are for really stupid people, or people who are much, much older and can deal with messy things like emotional attachments.

Also, Madison Allesio is now stalking me. When I say stalking, I mean it in relative terms. She's dropped the hard-to-get act, and is now making it pretty clear she wants to hook up. She's doing this by leaving me MySpace messages and texts that say "I want to hook up." The weird thing is, this shouldn't really be a problem. Because I don't even really want to hook up with her anymore. Which is why I probably should. Because if I don't, it means I'm emotionally attached to Courtney. And I can't have that.

This is what I'm thinking about as I'm driving to Courtney's house to do the math assignment. We usually do our math homework together in her room, which entails us doing a problem and then making out for a few minutes. Then she stops and says, "Jordan, we really have to do our work," and then we do two more problems and make out again for a while. It takes a lot longer to do the assignment this way, and yet the time seems to go by much faster.

The other thing that worries me about the Courtney situation is that I'm obviously spending so much time over there in an effort to avoid what's going on at my house. My strategy, as with most things, has been denial and avoidance. I just deny and avoid. The weird thing is, my parents don't seem to notice.

"What's up?" Courtney asks when I get to her house.

"Not much," I say. She leans into me as I pass by her on the way into the house, and I inhale her scent. She smells so good. Like . . . I don't know, exactly. Like Courtney.

Two hours later, we're making out on her bed. Our math books are on the floor. My hands are in her hair, and on her face, and under her shirt on her back. Her tongue is in my mouth, and I want her so bad.

"Wait," she says, pulling away. She pushes her hair away from her face and looks at me seriously. "I don't know what's going on here." She sits up and smoothes down her shirt.

Uh-oh. This is not good. This sounds like it's going to be a talk. Talks, as a rule, are not good. They usually mean something bad is going to happen. When bad things happen, I just like them to happen. Why waste time talking about them? Or about the possibility that they *could* happen? Again, denial and avoidance is really a great strategy, and saves everyone a lot of trouble.

"What do you mean?" I ask. I kiss her neck in an effort to distract her. "Your skin is so soft."

"Jordan," she says, pushing me away. "Stop. Seriously." Whoa. Okay. I pull away from her and back up against the wall behind her bed.

"I just . . ." she trails off. "I don't want to be a typical girl, but I need to know what's going on."

"Okay," I say slowly, not sure what to say. Not because I'm being forced to confront the issue, but because I really don't know what to tell her. I've been in this situation a lot before. Usually, girls aren't so vocal about it. You can just kind of tell they're getting to the point where they're going to press you for an answer about what's going on. They want you to be their boyfriend, not just a hookup. Which is fine, I can't blame them. I'm kind of a catch. Usually, I tell them I'm just not up for it. Sometimes they hate me. Sometimes we keep hooking up (although it's never the same). But this time, I realize I don't want to tell Courtney that I don't want to be her boyfriend. In fact, I do want to be her boyfriend. If that's even what she's saying.

"What are you saying?" I ask.

"I don't know," she says slowly. She looks down at the bed and traces her finger around a blue flower on her comforter. "It's just, I mean, I don't need you to be my boyfriend or anything." Oh. "But I just . . . I mean, what exactly is going on here?"

"Well," I say, running my hand through my hair. "I don't know. I love spending time with you, and I love being around you." I realize she's two feet away from me, and that makes me nervous. I reach out and touch her hand, and start drawing little circles with my index finger against her palm. I try to pull her close to me, but she resists.

"It just feels kind of weird to be spending all this time together and doing all the stuff we're doing without figuring out exactly what this is." She bites her lip. I lean over and kiss her. "Jordan, seriously," she says, pushing me away.

"Okay," I say, backing away. "Sorry. So, what do you want? Let's be together. Me and you." I kiss her again. I can't help it. "Be my girlfriend."

"Jordan, I'm being serious," she says. She rolls her eyes and pushes me away.

"So am I." I pull her close and look into her eyes. "Let's be together."

She leans her head against mine. "Is that really what you want?" she asks. She tilts her head up toward mine.

"Yes," I say.

"Because you shouldn't say it unless, you know, you really mean it. I don't want you to think you have to."

"I don't feel like I have to do anything," I say. I inch my lips closer to hers.

"Okay," she says. "So . . ."

I kiss her then, and she finally stops talking.

Three hours later, we're finally done with our math assignment. It was ten problems. Ten problems took us three hours. It's ten at night. I'm going to have no time to finish the rest of my homework. I hope having a girlfriend doesn't mess with my ability to keep my grades up. Ha.

"I should go," I say, trying to distangle myself from Courtney's body. We're laying in her bed, kissing, and I can't stop. It's like I'm physically unable to be away from her.

"Okay," she says, not moving. She closes her eyes for a second, and I try to memorize the way she looks, her hair spread out around the pillow, her lips slightly parted. She sighs and pulls herself out of bed, then holds her hand out, and pulls me up. I pull her close to me and kiss her again.

"I'll walk you to the door," she says when she pulls away.

"'Kay." I gather my stuff, shove it all into my black messenger bag, and walk with Courtney down the stairs.

As we're walking into the kitchen, the back door opens.

"Dad?" Courtney asks. Shit. Courtney's dad has been on a business trip for the past few weeks, so I haven't had to meet him. I hate meeting dads. Dads, as a rule, don't like me. They think I'm a punk who's trying to deflower their precious daughter. Which is usually the case. But not in this instance. Although I wouldn't mind deflowering Courtney, I'm content with the whole making-out thing. Maybe it wouldn't even be a deflowering. We haven't had the whole "Are you a virgin?" talk yet.

The back door opens and Courtney's dad walks in.

"You're home!" She flings herself at him and grabs him in a hug. This is going to be doubly disastrous, because Courtney and her dad are superclose. Which means getting his approval is key to our relationship. I use their reunion time to smooth my clothes and run my fingers through my hair. I hope I don't look like I've just been making out with his daughter.

"Jordan," Courtney says. "Come meet my dad." She pulls back, still holding his hand.

"Nice to meet you, sir," I say, holding out my hand. I get my first good look at him, and then stop. Because Courtney's dad is the guy my mom was making out with on the couch.

"Let me get this straight," B. J. says a couple hours later, leaning back in the booth. We're in Denny's, having a late-night snack, and I've just finished telling him the whole sordid tale. Everything. My mom. Courtney. Her dad. Everything. "Courtney is now your girlfriend."

"Right."

"And two hours after you two crazy kids came to the conclusion that you're soul mates, you figured out your mom was fucking her dad."

"Right." I don't even wince at B. J.'s crude language. I'm beyond that.

"Dude, that shit is FUCKED UP." He takes a fry and drags it through some ketchup. "What are you doing to do?"

"I have to tell her," I say. Silence. "Right?"

"Right," B. J. says, sounding uncertain.

"Why do you sound uncertain?"

"I don't," he says, sounding even more uncertain than before.

"Yes, you do!"

"Well, it's just one of those things that sounds good in theory, but might not really be necessary." He takes the straw out of his drink and throws it on the table, then takes a long gulp of his soda right from the cup. On cue, the waitress comes over and replaces his old soda with a new one.

"Thanks," B. J. says, grinning at her.

"You're welcome," she says, looking at me. "Do you need anything else?"

"No, I'm fine," I say, slightly annoyed that she's interrupting.

"You sure?" she persists. "Dessert? Coffee?"

"Nah, I'm good," I say, looking away and hoping she'll get the message.

"Oooh, you know what?" B. J. says, looking excited. "I'll have a piece of that strawberry thing, the one with all the whipped cream?" I resist the urge to hurl myself across the table and strangle him.

"Okay," she agrees. "Vanilla ice cream?"

"Sure," B. J. says. He shrugs. "Do it up."

"I'll bring two spoons." As soon as she clears the area, B. J. takes another gulp of his soda. He leans back in his chair and lets out a huge burp.

"Anyway," I say, trying not to freak out. "Can you please tell me why I shouldn't tell her?"

"Dude," B. J. says. He pulls an ice cube into his mouth and starts crunching it.

"Dude what?"

"Hold on," he says. "I'm trying to think of how to phrase this." Great. We'll be here all day.

"Don't try to think about how to phrase it," I say. "Just say it."

"You sure?"

"Yes!"

"You probably won't be with her for that long." He shrugs. "So there's really no point in telling her."

"Geez, tell me how you really feel."

"You said to just say it!"

"I know, I know," I say. I lean over the table and rub my temples with my fingers. Maybe B. J.'s right. Maybe I don't have to tell her. Maybe I can wait a little while until I figure out how I feel about her and then I can decide whether or not to tell her. I do like Courtney, I like her a lot, I don't want to hang out with anyone else, but I am fickle. What if I tell her and it wrecks her life? What if she's not supposed to know about this, and not only do I tell her, but otherwise, she never would have found out? It's not like my mom is planning on marrying her dad. I don't think, anyway.

"Dude, are you stressin' about this?" B. J. asks. "Don't freak me out."

"Why would that freak you out?"

"Because you never stress."

The waitress returns with a huge plate of strawberry pie, ice cream, and whipped cream. She sets down two spoons.

"I made a double portion," she says, smiling. She licks her lips and smoothes her hands across her tight apron. Lovely. My world is falling apart, and some random waitress is making threesome jokes. She walks away, swinging her hips from side to side. If I wasn't so fucked up right now, I'd probably be turned on.

"Dude," B. J. whispers, leaning across the table. "Does she want to have a threesome with us?"

"Probably."

"Whoa." His eyes widen. "Not that I ever would. No offense, bro, but that would be way too fucked up." He takes a bite of strawberry pie. "That is some good shit. Try it."

"No, thanks," I say. I'm suddenly not very hungry, and

the cheeseburger and fries I just devoured feel heavy in my stomach.

"You need to chill," B. J. says. He has whipped cream all over his mouth. I reach across the table and wordlessly hand him a napkin. He smiles sheepishly and wipes his mouth. "For now, you can't worry about it. The last thing you want to do is get Courtney all freaked out for nothing. And if you do decide it's going to turn into something serious, you can always tell her later."

"What if she asks why I didn't tell her before?"

"You can tell her the truth. That you wanted to make sure you knew what was going on between you guys, and between your parents, before you did anything psychotic." I stare at B. J. in disbelief. How is it that someone who is so idiotic most of the time can somehow be able to give such good insight? Maybe it's because he thinks on such a simple level most of the time that he doesn't get bogged down by things like emotion and manipulation. He just figures out the best way to handle a situation, and then he does it.

"Good idea," I say. "Thanks."

"No problem." He grins at me through a mouthful of strawberries.

"Anything else I can get you two?" the waitress says, appearing at our table.

"Just the check," I say. "Thanks."

She rips it off the pad slowly and places it down in front of me. "If you need anything else, I can always add it." She smiles again, turns on her heel, and walks away.

"You could so do her," B. J. says.

I pick up the check. $15.65. "Carrie," it says on the bottom. "Call me, cutie! 555-0181." Followed by a smiley face.

I throw a $20 down on the table and leave the check where it is.

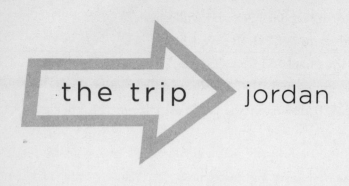

the trip ▷ jordan

Day Two, 11:37 a.m.

I'm probably going to get into a fight with Lloyd when we get to Middleton. That bitch has had it coming for a long time, and I couldn't be blamed for fucking him up. He never took the relationship I had with Courtney seriously. Even when we were together all the time, he'd still make little digs. Case in point: One night, when Lloyd, Court, me, B. J., Jocelyn, and a few other people were hanging out, Courtney decided she wanted to order food. And Lloyd was all, "Oh, Courtney, you always have to order food while we're watching baseball." Which may have been true. But it was the way he said it that pissed me off. It was like he was talking about food, but he basically was saying, "Jordan, I know Courtney better than you, and I could fuck her if I wanted to."

Anyway, we're in the car on our way to see my brother, Adam, and Lloyd at Middleton, and Courtney's acting like it's the night before Christmas. She's practically taking her clothes off already. I'm not stupid. I know some of it is an act, something she's probably doing to piss me off, but still. They hooked up. There has to be something there, or else she's one hell of an actress.

So far, she's asked me how her hair looks about five million times. She's wearing a black flippy skirt and a black tank top. Her hair is in pigtails, which you think would be kind of silly, but on her looks really cute. I've hardly ever seen Courtney dressed like this. She usually isn't so, uh . . . revealing.

"Does my hair look okay?" she asks again, flipping down the visor and checking herself out in the mirror.

"Yes," I say through gritted teeth. "Your hair looks fine."

"Sorry if I'm being annoying," she says, pulling a lip gloss out of her bag and lining her lips. "I'm just nervous."

"Understandable," I say, watching her out of the corner of my eye. She has the best mouth. I stare straight ahead again, keeping my eyes on the road.

"I'm starving," she announces. "Are we going to stop for breakfast or something?"

"Do you think that's smart, with your stomach and everything?" The last thing I need is Courtney throwing up all over my car again. Not that I really cared yesterday. I actually liked taking care of her. But things are different now. Yesterday she was cute and vulnerable. She wrapped her legs around me in bed, and pulled me close to her during the night. Now she's dressed like a tramp and thinking about having sex with Lloyd. So forgive me if I'm not rushing to hold her hair back. Let Lloyd do that shit if she's so into him.

"I'm hungry." She shrugs and pulls out the CD in the player and tosses it into the backseat. She pushes the button for the satellite radio and turns it to the country station.

"Feel free," I say, rolling my eyes. My phone starts vibrating in my pocket, and I do my best to ignore it.

"Your phone's ringing," Courtney says helpfully.

"Thanks," I say.

"You should answer it." She starts humming along to the song on the radio, something about someone's last days on earth and taking advantage of them. I'm about to go crazy listening to this country radio bullshit. Country is so depressing. There's too many slow songs. Why am I putting up with this shit? It's my car. I'm driving. I should be able to listen to whatever the fuck I want. Especially now that she's banging Lloyd. Let him put up with her country music bullshit, and her throwing up.

"Fine," I say. "I will." I pull my phone out of my pocket and make a big show of answering it.

"Hello?" I say, sounding upbeat, and like I'm happy to be on the phone. I decide to pretend it's my imaginary girlfriend. Fuck pretending to be nice.

"Yo," B. J. says.

"What's going on, honey?" I say, trying to glance at

Courtney out of the corner of my eye without her noticing that that's what I'm doing. She's going through her bag, probably looking for more makeup, so she can make herself look good for Lloyd.

"Honey?" B. J. asks. "Jordy, I had no idea you felt that way about me. I have to warn you, though, I happen to be in a very committed relationship."

"Yeah, I miss you, too." Courtney starts flipping through the satellite radio stations. Good. I hope she's rattled. I hope she realizes that if she weren't hooking up with Lloyd, I would let her pick any song she wanted to listen to. And that I would not be pretending to talk to my fake girlfriend.

"I'm guessing I'm your fake girlfriend?" B. J. asks, sighing. It's a miracle that he figured it out. He's not usually the best with things that aren't spelled out for him.

"Of course, sweetie," I say. I try not to think about the fact that I'm talking to B. J. like we're in love. B. J. is six-foot-four and 220 pounds. Not someone you want to think about being intimate with. Out of the corner of my eye, I see Courtney pull her iPod out of her bag and shove the headphones into her ears. I'm not buying it. I know she doesn't have the thing on. No way she doesn't want to hear me talk to my new girlfriend.

"Listen, I'm sorry to bother you when you're obviously busy with, uh, important things," B. J. says. He sounds sarcastic. "But you remember a few months ago, when we scored that pot for Brian Turner?"

"Sort of," I say, wondering if it would be going too far to call B. J. "pookie" or "schmooper." I want Courtney to be jealous, but I also don't want her thinking I'm a pussy. Which is really fucked up, since, you know, *I'm* the one that broke up with *her.*

"We paid for that, right?"

"Yeah," I say. A couple months ago we bought some pot for Brian Turner's party. It was this long, drawn-out procedure, since the first guy we were supposed to get it from wasn't where he was supposed to be, and then this guy named Gray Poplaski, who somehow ended up coming along even though he's kind of a tool, said he knew this other guy who could probably get us some. Which annoyed me, because I don't even like pot that much. Anyway, we finally met up with some very shady-looking guys and got it, but the whole experience was weird.

"Do you think anyone found out about that?" B. J. asks, sounding nervous.

"Found out about what?" I ask, trying to imagine why I would say that to my fake girlfriend. Maybe if she asked "Do you think anyone found out about that?" meaning, "Do you think anyone found out about us having sex in my parents' bed?" or something. I hope Courtney is smart enough to infer that that's what is probably going on. I wonder if it would be going too far to actually come out and say, "You mean about the doggie-style we had?"

"Found out about the pot we bought!" B. J. says, sounding exasperated. He's been sounding exasperated with me a lot lately. Which, like I said before, really worries me. Because if B. J. thinks you can't keep up, it probably means you're in deep shit.

"Like who?"

"I don't know," he says, lowering his voice. *"Like their posse."*

"Like whose posse?" I realize I probably won't be able to keep up pretending that I'm talking to my fake girlfriend for long, so I fake a call waiting beep. "I have to go," I say to B. J., a.k.a. my fake girlfriend (M.F.G.). "I have a beep." I pretend to mess around with the phone for a minute. "Hello? Oh, hi, B. J." I glance over at Courtney, hoping she now thinks that I was on the phone with my fake girlfriend until B. J. beeped in.

"Are you done?" B. J. asks, sounding annoyed.

"I think so."

"Anyway, their posse," B. J. says. "Could be after me."

"Whose posse?" I repeat, hoping Courtney doesn't notice that I appear to be having the same conversation with B. J. that I was just having with my fake girlfriend.

"Those thugs we bought it from!" B. J. says.

I'm starting to get a headache. "I'm starting to get a headache," I say.

"Look, I think someone's been following me," B. J. says. "And the only thing I can think of is that it might have something to do with that pot we bought."

"Someone's following you?" I ask. "Where are you?" I merge onto the freeway, and try to fight myself through the traffic. I really should put my phone on speaker, but I obviously can't, because then Court will know I've been talking to B. J. and not M.F.G. I have a headset in the glove compartment, but that would involve reaching over Courtney. Or asking her to pass it to me.

"I'm driving to the gym," he says. "And there's a car behind me, weaving in and out of traffic. I think I saw it yesterday, too."

"You're being paranoid." A red Jetta on my left side veers into my lane, and I swerve to avoid hitting it. My cell phone drops to the floor. Shit. I grope around on the ground while trying to get my car back into its lane. This is extremely dangerous.

"—and shoots me or something," B. J. is saying by the time I get the phone back to my ear.

"What?"

"What the fuck is going on over there? My shit is about to get BLOWN UP, and you're playing some kind of fucking game!" he says.

"Hold on one second." I put the phone into my lap. "Courtney," I say sweetly. "Can you reach into the glove compartment and hand me my cell-phone headset?"

She ignores me and pretends to be listening to her iPod.

"Court?" I say, raising my voice. From the depths of the cell phone in my lap, I can faintly hear B. J. saying "Hello?

Are you there? Jooorrrddaannn!" I flip the cell phone over, to muffle B. J.'s voice.

"COURTNEY!"

"Someee hearts just get luucccky sometimesss," she sings, her voice totally off-key. I'm in the midst of three lanes of high-speed traffic, have a friend on my cell phone who is obviously losing his mind, am faking phone calls, and am listening to my ex-girlfriend, who I'm still in love with, sing country songs. I really, really need to get off of this trip.

"Court." I poke her. She ignores me. I poke her harder.

"WHAT?!" she screeches, pulling her earphones out of her ears. "What do you want?"

"Can you reach into the glove compartment and hand me my cell phone headset, please?" I ask.

From my cell phone comes the faint sound of B. J. screaming. I pick it up and reduce the volume. Courtney sighs and reaches into the glove compartment like it's some huge imposition. She makes a big show of rummaging through the stuff until she locates the headset. Such a drama queen.

She hands it to me. "Thanks, honey," I say, and give her a wink. She rolls her eyes and puts the earphones of her iPod back into her ears. Like she's really listening to it.

"THIS SHIT IS FUCKED UP!" B. J. is screaming once I get the headset in.

"Sorry, I'm here," I say.

"What were you doing?"

"I was getting my headset so I could talk to you," I say. "Now, what's going on?"

"I. Am. Being. Followed. Like I said before."

"Are you sure?" I ask.

"Yes," he says. "There is a car following me. It followed me yesterday, too. It's those thugs from the drug deal, probably. Or maybe those fuckers we beat from Westhill."

"Maybe you should call the police," I say.

"I will not," he replies indignantly. "I'm not afraid of a gang. Or some shitty football team. I'll call my boys."

"Okay," I say uncertainly.

"Call ya back," he says and then disconnects.

"What's going on?" Courtney asks from the passenger seat. Oh, now she's concerned.

"Nothing," I say. "B. J. thinks he was being followed."

She looks startled. "Oh," she says. "Uh, by who?"

"Not sure."

"What's he going to do?"

"Call the police, I guess," I say, shrugging. No way I'm telling her about the gang violence and the fact that we bought drugs. She'd flip out, especially since we were together at the time. A worried look crosses her face, but she doesn't say anything.

"Can we PLEASE stop and get some food?" she asks five minutes later. "I'm starving."

I want to make a snide comment about how she wants to

eat so she'll have energy for her and Lloyd's impending sex-
a-thon, but I don't. I also want to point out that the schedule doesn't call for this kind of stop, but whatever.

"Geez, Jordan," she says. She pulls her lip gloss out of
her bag and starts relining her lips. "Could you be a worse
driver?"

I clutch the steering wheel and concentrate on not losing
my temper. I've decided passive aggressive is my new tactic.
But five minutes later, when Courtney looks at me pointedly
as we come up on the next exit, I put on my signal and pull
off the highway.

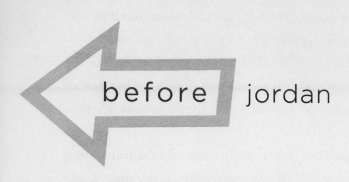

before jordan

77 Days Before the Trip, 6:07 p.m.

Courtney's dad is onto me. We're having dinner out at a Greek restaurant, and I can tell he wants to kill me. Okay, so he doesn't want to kill me, but he knows I know he's banging my mom.

"You have to try the souvlaki," Courtney says, reaching across the table and taking my hand. I hold her hand, trying not to freak out. Jesus, this is awkward. Definitely on my top ten list of things I don't ever want to do. "Number Three: Have dinner with your girlfriend and her dad, when said dad is having an extramarital affair with your mom, which your girlfriend doesn't know about." It really should be some sort of list on *Letterman*. "Top Ten Things You Never Thought About Happening, But Should Try to Avoid at All Costs."

"That sounds good," I say. I have no fucking idea what souvlaki is. It sounds disgusting. But I'll try it, because

Courtney's dad is here, and he's from Greece, and I'm trying to make a good impression.

"I hope you're hungry, Jordan," he says, smiling at me across the table. That's the other weird thing. He's acting like nothing is wrong. I wonder if maybe he has no idea who I am. But that would be impossible. He knows my last name. And he saw me the night I came in and found him feeling up my mom. Maybe he doesn't know my mom's last name. And maybe that night he was just so intent on banging her that he doesn't really remember what I look like. Maybe they haven't talked since. Maybe they broke it off.

"I am hungry, sir," I say. Courtney rolls her eyes next to me. Of course I'm going to "sir" him. I have to kiss his ass for many reasons, not the least of which is that even though I haven't told her yet, I think I'm in love with his daughter.

Courtney's dad ("Call me Frank," he said when we got here—Frank! Ha, fat chance!) motions the waiter over and starts talking to him in Greek. I wonder if they're talking about taking me outside and doing away with me. I don't think the mob is in Greece, though. The Sopranos are definitely Italian.

"He's ordering appetizers," Courtney says, as if she's reading my mind. She's wearing a black skirt and a long-sleeved pink shirt, and when she leans in close to me, I can see the black bra she's wearing underneath it. Despite all the stress, I feel myself starting to get turned on.

The waiter turns to me and asks me in a thick Greek accent what I'd like. I order the souvlaki since Courtney recommended it, and since she said it, I already know how to pronounce it.

"Salad?" the waiter asks, smiling. He's about twenty-two and he looks like he's in pretty good shape, but I know I could take him. If it came down to that.

"Yes, please," I say, figuring salad is safe. Salad is good. Salad is just lettuce. With dressing. Although maybe it's some kind of funky Greek salad. Even so, Greek lettuce is better than some unknown shit. I've never thought of myself as a picky eater before, but now I realize it's basically because I subsist on hamburgers and pizza most of the time. I'm probably going to die before I'm thirty.

"Whachu leek feetaumbla dreez?" the waiter says. At least, that's what it sounds like he says. Who the fuck can tell with his accent? Courtney and her father look at me expectantly. Fuck.

"What kind of dressing do you have?" I ask, proud of myself for inferring that was probably the question he asked.

"No," Courtney says, squeezing my hand and trying not to smile. "He asked if you want feta cheese. On your salad. They only have one kind of dressing here, the Greek house dressing."

"Oh," I say, shrugging. "Sure, I'll take the feta." I have no idea what feta cheese is.

Courtney and her dad give their orders, and the waiter clears the menus and leaves.

"So," Courtney's dad says. He picks up a piece of pita bread and dips it in some kind of cream that's sitting next to it. He pops it in his mouth and chews. I have no idea how the dude can be so calm, given what's going on right now. "I hear you're going to BU, Jordan."

"Yes, sir," I say. I wonder who he heard it from — Courtney or my mom. Although I'm not sure how comfortable my mom should feel talking about my life right now, since I haven't talked to her in weeks. For all she knows, I've scrapped this BU idea and have decided to head to Vegas and become a professional poker player. "That's wonderful," Frank says, smiling like it's anything but. He hates me.

The waiter sets our salads down in front of us, and I realize very quickly that the whole feta cheese thing was a horrible mistake. It looks gross and it smells gross, like old socks. And it's in chunks. I don't like anything that's in chunks. Chunks remind me of unpleasant things. Like vomit.

"Jordan's majoring in accounting," Courtney says in an effort to make me look good. In actuality, I'm going in undeclared, but I'm leaning toward accounting. I have no idea why, other than my dad is an accountant, and I feel like I need to do something to make him happy now that it turns out my mom is cheating on him.

"Nice," Frank says. He takes a bite of his salad, including

a piece of feta. "This cheese is unbelievable. How's your salad, Jordan?"

"It's really good, thanks," I say. And it is really good. Except for the cheese. And except for the fact that I have no appetite.

"You're not eating the cheese," Frank says accusingly.

And you're fucking my mom, I want to say back. But I don't. I take a bite of the cheese. It falls apart in my mouth. I try to swallow it without tasting it, like a pill, and almost choke.

"You okay?" Courtney asks, handing me my water.

"Yeah," I say. "I'm fine."

"So tell me more about this Miami trip," he says, looking right at me. "Courtney says you two are planning to go next month."

"Yes, sir," I say, trying to convey in those two words that we are going to hang out only, not to have sex ever. Which is true. I'm not expecting sex at all. Not even a little bit. Okay, so I'd be happy if it happened, but I'm not planning on it. Courtney's a virgin. As far as I know, she wants to stay a virgin. At least for a little while, anyway.

"And where will you be staying?" he asks, looking at me closely.

"My dad's best friend from college has a house there," I say, wondering if he's going to give me shit about the fact that there will be no parental supervision. "And he goes to Europe for the summer, and lets me use the house whenever I want."

"How generous of him. It sounds like it's going to be a fun trip," he says, shooting me a look over the table that basically means, "If you put a hand on my daughter, I will shoot you." Which really isn't fair, since he's feeling free to feel up my mom at any opportunity.

"Yes, sir," I say. I sound like a broken record.

"I'll be right back," Courtney says. She pushes her chair back from the table and stands up.

"Where are you going?" I ask, suddenly panicked. Why would she leave me alone with her father? Is Courtney insane?

"To the bathroom," she says. She kisses me on the forehead and then disappears.

Once she's cleared the area, Frank looks at me like I'm a piece of gum on his shoe.

"Listen, Jordan," he says. "This situation is only as difficult as you decide to make it."

"What do you mean?" I ask. Who does he think he is? Some kind of threatening hit man? Or Dr. Phil, warning me that I have my fate in my hands? I push the feta cheese around my salad with my fork, resisting the urge to throw it at him.

"I mean that this doesn't have to be an issue," he says. He wipes his lips with his napkin and sets it on the table. "I have no problem with you, Jordan. I have no problem with you seeing my daughter. The only problem we're going to have is if you decide not to be discreet."

Decide not to be discreet? Is this guy for real? The word "discreet" sounds so gross, like some kind of ad for hookers. I might not be pleased with my mom right now, but she's definitely not a hooker.

"I don't know what you're talking about," I say, just to be a dick. I start taking the feta cheese off my salad and dropping it onto my bread plate.

"Yes, you do," he says easily. "And I want you to know that I'm going to be the one to tell Courtney and her mom what's going on. Not you."

"You seem really sure of that," I say, continuing to throw the feta cheese onto the bread plate, spearing each piece and pretending it's Frank's head.

"I am," he says. "Because if Courtney finds out from you, I'll make sure you never see her again. Hell, I won't have to make sure of it. She'll hate you for keeping it a secret from her for this long."

I don't say anything because I know he's right. I had my chance to tell Courtney when I first found out her dad was the one who was having an affair with my mom, and I didn't. And now, because she had this preconceived notion that I was kind of a dick, if I tell her now, it's going to come off like I *am* a dick. But maybe . . . maybe if I keep my mouth shut, if I don't tell her I knew, if her dad does eventually tell her, we can deal with it together. We can help each other through it.

"Whatever," I say. "I'm not going to tell her."

"Good," Frank says. He takes a bite of his salad and licks the dressing off his lips. "I really do think that's the best way."

"Hey," Courtney says, returning to the table. "What'd I miss?"

before jordan

76 Days Before the Trip, 10:10 a.m.

"I think I might be in love with her," I tell B. J. in unstructured on Thursday morning. It's the last day of school, and we're sitting in the library, going over the review sheet for our AP Bio final.

"You are not in love with her," B. J. says. He leans back in his chair and rubs his temples.

"I am," I say. "I'm in love with her. I haven't told her yet, but I've been thinking it." It's true, too. Over the past two months we've gotten really close, and in the past month, I've started to think it. There have even been a couple times, especially when we're getting off the phone at night, or when I'm leaving her house that I want to say it. But I haven't yet, because I'm not sure if she feels the same way, and I don't want to freak her out.

"That is insane," B. J. says. "You can't be in love with her."

"Why not?"

"A myriad of reasons," B. J. says. I try to keep in mind this is the same guy who was dressed as a leprechaun the night he first hooked up with his girlfriend.

"Such as?"

"You haven't had sex."

"So?"

"So, sex is very important to a relationship," he says. "How do you know you love her if you haven't had sex with her?"

"Not even dignifying that with a response," I say. The weird thing is, even though Courtney and I haven't had sex, I haven't thought that much about it. I mean, I have thought about having sex with her, of course, and I definitely want to, but I haven't thought much about the fact that we're not having it. It's just something I figure will happen when it happens. Courtney's a virgin, so obviously I'm not going to rush it.

"Okay," B. J. says. He leans back in his chair and stretches his arms behind him. "How about the fact that you weren't supposed to get attached to her? Dude, her dad is banging your mom. If she finds out you kept that from her, you are so fucked."

"I'm sure she'll understand," I say, a knot of uneasiness starting in my stomach. She won't understand. Courtney has this thing about trust. And if she knows I lied to her, she'll break up with me immediately.

"Dude, you have to tell her," B. J. says. "I would never keep something like that from Jocelyn."

I resist the urge to roll my eyes. B. J. and Jocelyn hooked up more or less around the same time Courtney and I did, but for some reason, I get super annoyed when he tries to imply that the relationships are the same. From what I can tell, he and Jocelyn have sex a lot. As in, every single day. Sometimes multiple times. They spend a lot of time together, but they don't really do anything. Except have sex. I've never even really seen them talk. Unless they're setting a time to meet up later so they can have sex.

The bell rings and we file out of the library and into the hall. "I know I have to tell her," I say. "But her dad is freaking me the fuck out."

"Don't be afraid of that shit-sucker," B. J. declares. "You need me to have a talk with him?"

"Nah," I say. "I'll figure it out." But as I leave B. J. in the hall and walk in to take my English final, I have no idea how I'm going to do that.

courtney before

76 Days Before the Trip, 12:23 p.m.

"You had sex with him?" I say to Jocelyn, trying not to spit out my Sprite. Why she would wait until I took a drink to announce she had sex with B. J. is beyond me. Maybe because it's the last day of school. So she feels the need to start the summer with a huge confession.

"When did this happen?"

"You mean when was the first time?" she asks, frowning.

"There's been more than one time?" Is it possible she means more than one time in one night? Don't boys need time to, uh, recharge? Not that I would really know much about that. The recharging, I mean. Or the sex in general.

"Yes," she says, then leans in conspiratorially, since we're in the cafeteria and all. "I think I might be a little addicted to it."

Great. My best friend is a sex addict. And not only that, she's addicted to doing it with B. J. Which is a mental

165

picture I'm really trying to keep out of my head. Not that B. J. is ugly or anything, but still. It's B. J.

"Well," I say. "I'm going to have sex with Jordan."

"Courtney!" Jocelyn exclaims. Her eyes widen and she puts down her fork, which she's been using to eat french fries off my tray. I have no idea why she doesn't just pick them up and eat them, but she won't. She spears them with a fork and then dips them in the little cup of ketchup that came with my lunch.

"What?" I ask.

"You cannot have sex with Jordan."

"Why not?" I ask. "I actually can. I mean, my body is capable of doing it." I think it is, anyway. Although I do remember reading somewhere that if you don't have sex for a while, your virginity actually grows back, and it can be hard for you to do it again. Not that that's my situation, since I haven't had sex before. But maybe if you wait too long, it gets harder to do it. But that's insane, right? Besides, I'm seventeen, not thirty.

"Well, of course your body is capable of doing it," Jocelyn says, rolling her eyes. She flips her hair over her shoulder and studies me seriously. "Courtney, you can't undo this. It's not like buying a new shirt."

"I know that," I say, rolling my eyes right back. "And the thing is, it doesn't scare me." It doesn't. I want to be with him. I love him.

"Oh, my God," Jocelyn says. "You love him."

"No, I don't," I say, as if the thought of me being in love with someone is so totally ludicrous. Which, in a way, it kind of is. Here's the weird thing—before I met Jordan, I kind of thought I would never be in love. Like, ever. It just seemed totally far-fetched that I would find a guy who would fall in love with me and take care of me and everything. But I did. I'm in love with him.

"You do!" Jocelyn says. "You love him. If you didn't, you wouldn't even be considering sleeping with him." Damn. That's what happens when you have a friend who knows you really, really well. You can't get away with pretending to be someone you're not.

"Does he love you?" she asks.

"I don't know," I say slowly, thinking about it. "I think he does."

"Think is not good enough, Court," she says. "Do you really want to sleep with someone if you don't know they love you?"

"It's not like that," I say, frowning. "I love him. Isn't that enough?"

"Not really," she says. "This is a huge decision, Courtney. You have to make totally sure this is what you want. Because it's something that's forever."

"What about you and B. J.?" I ask. "How come it's okay for you guys?" This sounds like a sex double standard. How come she's allowed to do it and I'm not? I'm not going to say anything, but sometimes I wonder if her and B. J. even really like each other. They never do anything except drink and make out. And now, apparently, have sex.

"Different situation," she says. She pulls a tube of lip gloss out of her purse and lines her lips. "Want some?" she asks, extending the tube to me. "It would be really cute on you."

I take it and dab a little on my lips, marveling at the fact that she can intersperse talking about sex with talking about lip gloss. How can she be so cavalier? Is this what happens after you have sex? You just talk about it like it's nothing? That makes me nervous for some reason, to think that something that's such a big deal now could end up being nothing in the future. Although I guess it's to be expected. Like, look at the girls on *Sex and the City*. They did it all the time.

"How is it a different situation?" I roll the lip gloss around my lips, wondering if it makes me kissable.

"Because we're different people," she says. "I don't know if you can separate the emotional from the physical."

"Why would I want to do that?" I ask, frowning. Who does that? Separates the emotional from the physical? I guess sociopaths, maybe. And I guess Jocelyn is now claiming to do it, too, although I never pegged her for a sociopath.

"Because if you don't, you could end up getting really, really hurt," she says. "Listen, I'm not trying to discourage you. But you just have to make sure this is what you want to do."

"It is," I say. And I really do feel like it is. I want to have sex with Jordan. And when we go to Miami next month, I'm going to.

the trip > courtney

Day Two, 1:31 p.m.

"Did you not hear me?" I hiss into the phone. "He's starting to talk law enforcement."

"I don't understand how this could have happened!" Jocelyn's annoyed. "I've been so careful."

"Well, apparently you haven't, because he told Jordan someone's been following him since yesterday, and that he was going to call the police." I'm sitting in Jordan's TrailBlazer at a Burger King right off our route. Jordan's inside using the bathroom and getting us food. I told him I wanted to wait in the car since it's raining, but really I wanted to call Jocelyn and warn her about B. J.'s revelation.

"You have to stop," I say. I look out the back window to see if Jordan is coming out of the restaurant yet, but I don't see him. "Stop right now."

"I can't stop yet!" Jocelyn says. "It's too early. Maybe I

could borrow my sister's car . . . Did he say how he figured out someone was following him? Maybe I just have to change my technique."

"I don't know how he figured it out."

"Can you ask him?"

"Ask who?"

"Jordan!"

"No, I can't ask him! What would I say? 'Can you tell me how B. J. found out he was being followed, because it was Jocelyn and she wants to know if she needs to switch cars or just change her stalking technique?'" Oh, my God. Jocelyn is delusional. This is exactly why hooking up with people is not a good idea. Once you've crossed that line it just makes you insane. You start doing things normal people would never, ever do. Where the hell is Jordan with the food? I'm hungry again. Which is weird. Is it possible that since I was throwing up all day yesterday, I'm trying to eat enough food for two days? Hmm.

"Maybe there's nothing going on," I say. "Maybe B. J. really is just going to the places he says he is."

"Courtney!" Jocelyn gasps. "Please tell me you are not that deluded! Guys are never doing exactly what they say they're doing."

"Why not?" I say. "Maybe some are doing exactly what they say they're doing."

She snorts. "Listen, do what you can," she says. "And let me know if B. J. calls back."

I hang up the phone and lean my head against the head-rest. We're about two hours away from Middleton and Lloyd, which is making me nervous. I'm trying to play it off to Jordan like I'm wicked excited, while inside I feel like I'm going to explode. I have no idea how this is going to go down.

The driver's-side door opens and Jordan gets into the car, juggling a drink carrier and two bags of food. I take one of the bags out of his hand.

"Thanks," he says. He sets the other bag down carefully between us, pulls my soda out of the carrier, and hands it to me.

"You needed two bags?" I ask incredulously. I peek inside and inhale the scent of the food. It smells good. And greasy. I love grease. Grease makes me happy. I am only going to eat half of my food, though. Just half. So that my stomach doesn't get all sketched out.

"No, but there was a mix-up and somehow I got someone else's order, too."

He shrugs and pulls out a container of fries.

"Did you tell them?" I ask without thinking.

"Of course I told them," he says, rolling his eyes. "They let me keep it." Right. I'll bet Mercedes or whatever the hell her name is doesn't question Jordan's morals when it comes to fast food that's been given to him.

"Cool," I say nonchalantly, shrugging my shoulders. Jordan's cell phone starts playing "Baby Got Back" again, and he ignores it.

"Going to answer that?" I ask.

"Nope," he says cheerfully. He opens a container of chicken tenders and pulls open the packet of honey mustard that comes with them. I hate honey mustard. It seems like such a bad idea. Honey and mustard together. Who could like that?

"You don't have to feel weird about answering it," I say. "I told you."

"I don't," he says. He takes a chicken tender and dunks it into the honey mustard. Something about that makes me sad. Because all the little things about him, like the way he loves honey mustard and the way he always forgets the cheese on my burger, aren't mine anymore. It's weird that everything can be the same, that he can go on liking honey mustard, and yet everything is different.

"So, uh, the whole B. J. thing," I say, trying to distract myself from my impending condiment sadness. Honey mustard is so not a good reason to be upset. Orphans in Africa, drunk drivers killing innocent people, even not getting into your safety school (for me it was Florida State) are all good reasons to get upset. Chicken tenders sauces are definitely not. I try not to think about it, and instead focus on the fact that Jocelyn is insane.

"What B. J. thing?" He reaches into the bag and pulls out a napkin. He wipes his hand with it and sets it on his lap.

"With him calling the police or whatever. Do you think he's really going to do that?"

"I dunno." His phone starts going off again, and my sadness over the honey mustard is suddenly annoyance that he won't answer the call. Why won't he answer it? It's either because he's trying to look cool by not or he's trying to protect my feelings. Does he really think I'm that upset by the whole breakup? I mean, I am, but I've given him no reason to think I would be. Have I? I wrack my brain, trying to determine if there's any way he could know how upset I am.

"Would you answer your phone?" I snap.

He reaches in his pocket, pulls it out, and makes a big show of turning it off.

I roll my eyes. "Whatever. Listen, we need to talk about the schedule." Our schedule is now completely screwed up. We were supposed to be in North Carolina by now.

"What about it?"

"It's all screwed up. We need to reevaluate it."

"It's not that screwed up." He shrugs. "We'll be at Middleton by tonight, and we'll leave tomorrow. Obviously we won't be able to visit for that long, but we won't be that far off the schedule."

Suddenly, I'm struck with a brilliant idea. Maybe I can convince Jordan that we can't stop at Middleton, because IT WILL MAKE US LATE FOR ORIENTATION. That would be perfect. I could call Lloyd, tell him that we can't make it because we're way behind schedule, and then I wouldn't have to deal with the whole thing.

"Well," I say slowly, pretending that I'm thinking about it. "Maybe we shouldn't stop."

"What?" Jordan asks, frowning. He takes another tender and dips it in the honey mustard. I resist the urge to reach over and take it out of his hands and throw it out the window. Honey mustard is obviously not good for my mental state.

"I just mean with the schedule the way it is and everything, it might be better if we just drove straight through."

"But it's not going to throw us off that much. If we don't stop, we'll actually be ahead of schedule."

God, why is he being such an ass? And since when is he such an expert on the schedule? He didn't even read the damn thing. Does he really need to contradict everything I say?

"Besides," he goes on, "I thought you'd be happy to see Lloyd."

Right. "I am," I say. "But we need to stick to the schedule, too." This should be a perfectly reasonable explanation. I mean, he knows I'm totally anal retentive.

My phone rings before I can come up with a better response, and I check the caller ID. Lloyd. Lovely.

"Aren't you going to answer that?" Jordan asks, grinning.

"Of course," I say, rolling my eyes.

"Hey," I say into the phone. "What's up?" I think "What's up?" is a very good, neutral phrase to be saying to Lloyd under the circumstances. Like, I could totally see myself saying it to a boyfriend, so Jordan will be convinced that something really is going on with Lloyd, but at the same time, it's also something you can say to a friend, so Lloyd won't be all, "Oh, wow, Courtney must be in love with me."

"Hey," Lloyd says. "I've been trying to call you for a while."

"Really?" I say, trying to sound innocent. I know he's been calling. I just turned my phone off.

"Yeah," he says. "It kept going right to voice mail."

"I don't know why," I say, still trying to sound innocent. "It's raining here, so . . ."

"It's raining where?" he says, sounding confused.

"Where we are," I say, trying to sound deliberately vague.

"What does that have to do with anything?"

"It may have been messing with my cell reception."

"I don't think that has anything to do with it, Courtney," he says. Well, duh. Why would rain be messing up my cell reception?

"I don't know," I say again. Jordan shifts on the seat next to me and takes a loud sip of his soda.

"You don't sound right," Lloyd says. "Is Jordan giving you a hard time?"

"Uh, no," I say, "He's not."

Jordan stops with a fry halfway to his mouth. "I'm not what?" he asks, frowning.

I shake my head at him and hold up my hand, trying to

act like it's not important. Which, true to what's been going on, makes him just want to know more. "What did he say?" Jordan demands. He reaches over and turns off the radio.

"Nothing," I mouth at him, and turn it back on. He turns it off. I turn it on. "Quit it," I say.

"What's going on?" Lloyd asks again through my phone.

"Nothing," I say to Lloyd. "We're just having a little problem with the radio. You know, because of the storm."

"You guys are listening to the radio?"

"Well, not right now," I say, which is true. Jordan's turned it off again, and now he's maneuvering his body, trying to get closer to me so that he can hear what Lloyd is saying.

"Not right now what?" Lloyd asks.

"We're not listening to the radio right now," I say. "Because we're having problems with it because of the storm. Jordan has satellite."

"Figures." Lloyd snorts. Lloyd hates the fact that Jordan is kind of spoiled. Which really makes no sense, because Lloyd himself is quite spoiled. In fact, his parents just bought him a brand-new Mustang for graduation. Which he can't even use, since he can't have a car at school. So now his brand-new car is just sitting in the garage, probably getting used by no one. I wonder if Lloyd would let Jocelyn drive his car. There's no way B. J. would recognize it.

"Anyway," I say. "I'm going to let you go now, but I'll call you when we get close."

Jordan, seeing that the conversation is about to end anyway, reaches over and moves the volume up to almost full blast. Rap music comes blaring out of the speakers.

I reach over and very calmly turn off the radio. "Jordan," I say, "would you please refrain from turning up the music like that when I'm on the phone? I'd really appreciate it."

"HELLO?" Lloyd says much too loudly, now that the radio is off.

"Yeah," I say. "Sorry about that."

"I don't understand why you guys are listening to music," Lloyd says.

"What do you mean?"

"I thought you were dreading this trip," he says.

"I was," I say. What does that have to do with listening to music?

"*Was* as in past tense?" Lloyd asks, sounding quite like a jealous boyfriend. I'm not stupid. I know Lloyd isn't jealous about me, per se, but more about the fact that I'm with Jordan.

"No," I say. "I am not having a fun time on this trip." I am still dreading it, although that really makes no sense, because there's nothing to dread anymore, since I'm in the middle of actually taking part in it.

"You're not having a good time?" Jordan asks, sounding surprised.

"Why does he sound surprised?" Lloyd asks.

"I am having a horrible time on this trip," I say to Lloyd. Which isn't exactly a lie. I mean, I've spend a good part of it with food poisoning, listening to Jordan talk to his new girlfriend, dealing with the fact that Jocelyn is possibly going to get a restraining order taken out against her, and listening to rap music. It's been bad. "Now I will call you when I get close."

"I can't wait to see you, Court," Lloyd says, his voice softening.

"I'm excited to see you, too," I say, a twinge of guilt rising up in me as I realize this might not exactly be the truth. But I don't know if it's exactly a lie, either. After all, even if this whole hooking-up thing doesn't work out, Lloyd has always been my friend. So it will be nice to see him and hang out. I click off my phone.

"You're having a horrible time?" Jordan asks, looking hurt.

"Can we not talk?" I say. I open the bag my food is in and pull out a french fry.

"Why not?" he asks, sounding hurt again. "Now we can't even talk?"

"No." I take a bite of my fry, which is now cold. Surprisingly, for some reason this makes it taste better. I love fast food. I take a sip of my diet Coke and eat another fry.

"We can't talk, ever, for the rest of this trip?"

"Yes, we can talk for the rest of this trip, I'm not stupid. I know it would be impossible to not talk for the rest of this trip."

"So what you're saying is we can talk, but we can't?"

"Look, it's not that hard to figure out," I say. "We can talk about normal things, like the route we're taking, the schedule, toll money, etc. But no, like, chatting." These fries are so good. I take out a packet of ketchup and look for somewhere to squeeze it. I hate ketchup directly on my fries. I'm definitely more of a dipper. Jordan hands me his empty chicken tender container wordlessly, and I squeeze the packet of ketchup into it.

"Thanks," I say.

"So thanking me is allowed?" he asks.

"Jordan, stop. You know what I mean."

"Oh, I'm sorry," he says. He sounds pissed. Why is he pissed?

"Why are you pissed?" I ask.

"I'm not pissed."

"Well, you look pissed. And you sound pissed."

"Well, I'm not."

"Okay," I say, knowing that he is. Jordan can never admit when he's pissed. I don't know why. It's like this thing, where if he admits to you that he's angry, he's lost or something. Although I think he's just that way with me. Or maybe with girls. I wonder if he's like that with his new girlfriend.

"I just don't think you should be listening to every little thing Lloyd tells you to do," he says.

"I'm not," I say.

"Okay," he says, not sounding like he means it.

"Seriously, I'm not. I just think it would be better if we don't talk much." I shrug.

"Because of Lloyd."

"Can you get off the Lloyd thing?"

"Why?"

"Because I already told you, it has nothing to do with Lloyd."

"Well, it's a little weird that you were fine until you talked to Lloyd, and now all of a sudden you don't want to talk to me."

I snort. Does he really think we were fine this whole time? Has he not noticed the fact that there is this very weird tension between us, due to the fact that he dumped me two weeks ago for some other girl?

"What?" he demands.

"Nothing," I say. "I think it's just kind of funny that you think we're fine."

"I don't see why we can't be," he says. "People break up and stay friends, Court."

"True," I say. "But I don't really want to be your friend." It's true. I don't want to be his friend. I want to be his girlfriend or nothing. I feel a lump rising in my throat and I take a sip of my soda in an effort to push it back down. I can feel Jordan watching me, so I open up the fast food bag and take out my Whopper. I peel off the paper and take a bite of the burger. He remembered the cheese this time. I look at the burger and promptly burst into tears.

the trip ▷ jordan

Day Two, 1:50 p.m.

"Dude, it's Jocelyn," I say, looking over my shoulder nervously, just waiting for Courtney to get out of the Burger King. Could this trip be any more fucked up? Seriously. Courtney bursts into tears, something about cheese on her burger (which I know I remembered, because I knew if I didn't, she was going to flip the fuck out). She ran into Burger King crying, and I stood outside the bathroom, yelling in to her and looking like a freak. She kept telling me to go away, so finally I did, and now I'm waiting in the car for her to come out. The weird thing is, all I can think about is that song by Digital Underground, the one with the lyric "I once got busy in a Burger King bathroom." I think I have it on a mix CD in here somewhere.

"This isn't Jocelyn," B. J. says, sighing. "It's Jordan. Dude, try to play a better trick than that. You sound nothing like her. Plus your number came up on my caller ID."

"No," I say, feeling like I'm living in some sort of weird alternate reality. "Jocelyn is the one who's following you."

"Why would Jocelyn be the one who's following me?" B. J. asks, sounding thoroughly confused. Again, I'm struck by his ability to be very insightful and smart about some things and then totally clueless about others. Maybe he's one of those idiot savants.

"Because she wants to know where you're going, obviously," I say. I crane my neck to get a look at the Burger King. Still no sign of Courtney. I'm giving her five more minutes, and then I'm going back in there. What is it with me and the women's bathroom?

"Why would she want to know where I'm going?" B. J. asks, sounding even more confused. "Wait, how do you even know this?"

"Because Courtney was asking all these questions about who was following you, and about how I should try to convince you not to call the police because it was probably nothing."

"So?"

"So obviously she was saying that because it's Jocelyn, and they don't want you calling the police and getting her in trouble, and/or finding out it's her."

"Did you just say 'and/or'?"

I don't respond.

"Why would Jocelyn be following me, though?" B. J. asks again. "She knows where I'm going. I tell her every second where I'm going to be. I check in."

"Maybe she doesn't believe you," I say. "Maybe she's following you because she wants to make sure you really are where you say you are."

"That's ridiculous," B. J. says. "Why would I lie about where I'm going?"

"She doesn't trust you," I tell him. "I have to go."

"Why wouldn't she trust me?" he demands. "I'm totally trustworthy."

I try not to point out that not only does B. J. tend to get caught doing things and then lie about them, he also has an extremely impulsive personality, which makes him do things spur of the moment. Like dress up as a midget. Or cheat on his girlfriend. Not that B. J. has ever cheated on Jocelyn. Not that I know of, anyway.

"Listen," I say, "I gotta go. But it's definitely Jocelyn. You should talk to her."

"Hmm," B. J. says, sounding unsure. I want to be a good friend, but I really can't deal with this right now. I slap my phone shut and head inside to rescue Courtney from a women's bathroom for the second time in twenty-four hours.

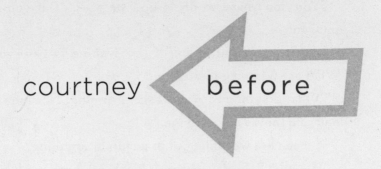

courtney before

33 Days Before the Trip, 6:57 p.m.

"This house," I say, "is amazing." I take a soda out of the refrigerator, pop the top, and pour half of it into my glass. I can't believe I'm in Miami. It feels exotic for some reason, just saying that.

"It is pretty awesome," Jordan says, sitting down next to me at the bar. I hand him my glass and he takes a sip of my drink.

"So what's this place like tonight?" I ask. Jordan, B. J., Jocelyn, and I are going to the beach, then out to dinner, and I want to make sure I'm dressed appropriately.

"What do you mean?" Jordan asks. He hands me back my soda.

"I mean, is it dress up or what?" I bought this amazing black dress that I can't wait for Jordan to see me in. It has a flowing, crinkly skirt and a low back.

"You don't have to dress up," he says. "But you can if you want."

"And what about after?" I say, leaning in close to him. "What are we going to do after?"

"What do you mean?" he asks, grinning. He shifts in his chair and moves closer to me.

"I mean are we going out to a club or anything?"

"A club?" Jordan throws his head back and laughs. "You want to go to a club?"

"Of course," I say. "Why wouldn't I?"

"Um, because you don't dance?"

Hmm. This is true. But I feel like dancing tonight. "We're in Miami," I say. "Isn't that what people do in Miami? Besides, I do so dance."

He raises his eyebrows.

"It's my new thing," I say. "Dancing is my new thing."

"Oh, really?" He leans in close to me and puts his forehead against mine. "Since when?"

"Jordan," I say, "are you trying to say I'm a bad dancer?"

"No," he says. "Of course not."

"Good," I say. "Need I remind you that my dancing was the thing that attracted you to me in the first place?"

He tilts his head to the side, then kisses me lightly on the lips. "That is true," he says. "You're a very hot dancer."

"I know," I say. "And tonight I'm going to be a dancing machine."

"Okay," he says, kissing me again. "But you have to promise you're not going to dance with anyone else."

"No one else?" I say. I cock my head to the side, pretending to consider. "But what if some really cute guy asks me to?"

"No," he says. He kisses me again, a little more forcefully again. "I want you all to myself."

"What about girls?" I ask, smiling. "Can I dance with girls?"

"Only if I can watch," he says, grinning.

"Eww," I say. "You're dirty." I push him playfully, but he grabs my arms, and this time, I kiss him. He kisses me back, and his hands are in my hair and on my face.

"We have to stop," he says, after a few minutes, pulling away. But I can't help but think about what would happen if we didn't stop, if we just kept on kissing, if we just kept going and didn't stop.

"I don't want to," I say, trying to pull him close to me again.

"We have to," he says, giving me another light kiss on the lips.

"We don't *have* to do anything," I say.

He laughs. "We're supposed to be going to the beach," he says. "With B. J. and Jocelyn, remember?"

"Yeah," I say, sighing.

"And if we don't go, they'll probably end up killing each other."

"True," I say. "I don't want to be responsible for the deaths of our friends."

"Then come on," he says. He holds his hand out, and I slide my palm into his. "But later," he whispers huskily, "you're mine."

You have no idea, I think. I follow him happily up the stairs to where Jocelyn and B. J. are waiting.

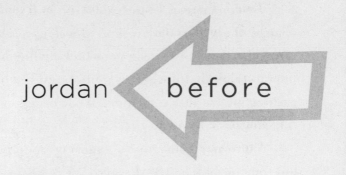

jordan before

33 Days Before the Trip, 7:07 p.m.

"Seriously, they do have naked beaches here," B. J. says, grinning. He's wearing camouflage shorts and a T-shirt that reads "Hi! You'll do."

"Perfect," Jocelyn says, pulling off the pink tank top she's wearing and exposing the top of her white bikini. "So you'll have no problem if I go topless."

"No problem at all," B. J. says, grinning again.

"Great," Jocelyn says. "So you'll have no problem with all the guys on the beach staring at me." She crosses her arms across her chest with a satisfied expression on her face. B. J. frowns, and Courtney and I look at each other nervously.

B. J. and Jocelyn are, at their best, volatile. They have this weirdness between them that tends to come out at horrible times. On prom night, they got in this huge fight in the limo about Katelyn Masters, a girl B. J. used to hook up

189

with freshman year. In the midst of the fight, B. J. went to change the radio station, and Jocelyn screamed, "If you touch that music I'll break your fucking fingers!" I'm beginning to think that Jocelyn is quite crazy, although Courtney assures me it's just something B. J. brings out in Jocelyn, that she's usually sane.

"You're not going to be exposing your boobs to every guy on the beach," B. J. says. We're all in Miami, at my dad's friend's house, standing in the room Courtney and I are sharing. We were getting ready to go out to the beach, and then B. J. made the remark about boobs, which has obviously put a kink in the plan.

"Why not?" Jocelyn asks. "You're so intent on seeing everyone else's boobs, and you're all excited about the naked beaches."

"So?" B. J. asks. He takes the baseball cap he's wearing off his head and throws it onto the bed, which is not a good sign. In my experience, when B. J. starts removing any kind of clothing, it can only lead to bad things.

"Actually," I say, "it's private beach property outside, so there probably won't be that many people around."

"So let's go! Do you have your sunscreen?" Courtney asks brightly. She pulls a bottle of Coppertone out of her bag and squirts some into her hand.

"I don't!" I say. "I don't have my sunscreen!" I'm almost shouting it. I sound like a tool, but it's what needs to be done if we want to save the situation. Otherwise, Jocelyn and B. J. are going to be fighting all night and ruining our good time.

"Jocelyn?" Courtney asks, holding up the bottle. "Do you need some sunscreen?"

"Yes," Jocelyn says calmly. "Actually, I do." Oh, thank God. Situation diffused. Score one for Jordan and Courtney.

"Here you go," Courtney says, holding out the bottle. Jocelyn takes it, then reaches behind her back, unhooks her bikini top, and starts slathering the lotion on her bare boobs.

"Jesus!" B. J. screams. "What the fuck are you doing?"

Courtney looks at me, and I quickly look away from Jocelyn's boobs.

"I'm getting ready for the beach!" Jocelyn says. I move to the other side of the bed and sit down facing the wall. The last thing I need is seeing my girlfriend's best friend's bare boobs. That can definitely not be good, especially since she's also my best friend's girlfriend. This whole thing is getting very incestuous, what with Courtney's dad banging my mom and everything.

"Um, I think we should go," Courtney whispers in my ear.

"Probably a good idea," I say.

"So, we're going to go," Courtney announces, as B. J. screams, "PUT THAT BACK ON IMMEDIATELY!"

We walk out of the room (OUR room, I might add— B. J. and Jocelyn have their own room, but of course they elected to start their naked fight in ours) and onto the beach.

Once we're settled into the sand, Courtney and I look at each other and start laughing.

"They are so fucked up," I say, leaning back on my towel. The sun is starting to set, which means there probably wasn't too much reason for sunscreen. "Good diversionary tactic with the sunscreen," I say.

"Thanks," she says, smiling. She's wearing a purple bikini and black sunglasses, and I reach over and pull her sunglasses off her eyes. "Come here," I say, pulling her close to me.

"I'm so glad we're not them," Courtney says, snuggling into my arm.

"Ya think?" I say, kissing the top of her head.

"They're so crazy," she says. "They're not honest with each other at all. It's like they almost get off on messing with the other person's head."

There's a sick feeling in my stomach when she says the word "honest" and I try to ignore it.

"Yeah," I say. "They're all screwed up."

"Not like us," she says, pushing me down on the sand. She gets on top of me and starts kissing my neck.

"Whoa, whoa," I say, turning away. Her long hair slides across my chest. "You want to make out on the beach?"

"There's no one around," she says, and I pop my head up and look down the beach. She's right. Way down, there's an old guy walking his dog, but they're moving in the opposite direction from us.

She starts kissing me again, on the mouth this time, and

my hands are in her hair and on her face. Every so often she pulls away and looks at me, and her eyes are the most beautiful thing I've ever seen. Then suddenly, she's looking at me intently and whispering something, and I'm so caught up in her that I don't hear what it is.

"What did you say?" I murmur into her hair. She slides her body off mine and settles in next to me.

"I said I want to be with you," she says into my chest.

"You are with me," I say.

"No, I mean, I want to make love to you," she says, and my eyes spring open. Whoa.

"Whoa," I say. I prop myself up on my elbow and look at her. "Court, that's . . ."

"I know," she says, smiling. "I know it's a big deal and all that. And Jordan, I've thought about it, I really have." I believe her, too. She's definitely an analytical sort of girl, and I know she wouldn't take something like this lightly.

"Are you sure?" I ask, dumbfounded. It's not that I don't want to. Believe me, I do. There are times when Courtney and I are doing our math homework and making out that I feel like I'm going to go insane from wanting her so bad. But anytime we've even talked about it, she's made it pretty clear that she wasn't ready.

"Yes," she says. "I'm sure." She frowns. "You don't want to?"

"Of course I want to," I say truthfully.

"Good." She starts kissing me again, and her tongue is in

my mouth and she tastes and feels so good, and I can feel her body pressing against mine and I'm so turned on that I almost lose my head.

"Wait," I say. "You want to do it right here?" How is this happening? Somewhere along the line, Courtney has become sex crazed, and now wants to have sex on the beach.

"If you want to," she says.

"You don't want your first time to be on a beach," I say.

"I don't care, as long as it's with you," she says, her face flushed. She starts kissing my neck. "Hey, Jordan?" She pulls away and looks right at me.

"Yeah?"

"I love you." She's looking in my eyes, and she's waiting for me to say it back, and I want to. I feel it. I do love her. But then I start thinking about her dad, and how I'm lying to her, and suddenly, I know I can't say it. I shouldn't say it.

"Thanks," I say, swallowing. A look of confusion crosses her face, and for a second, I don't think I'm going to be able to do it. But I look away from her before I can get caught up in the moment. "We should go inside." She climbs off me, and I still don't look at her, because I know I won't be able to take the look on her face. "And check on Jocelyn and B. J." I stand up and brush the sand off my shorts and start walking toward the house. And after a second, I can hear Courtney following me.

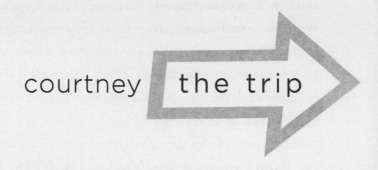

courtney **the trip**

Day Two, 2:37 p.m.

I'm having a breakdown in a random Burger King bathroom. This is upsetting for a few reasons, not the least of which is that it's happening in a bathroom. I mean, a breakdown at any time is not something that one should be excited about, but to have one in a public rest room is definitely doubly upsetting. And it's not even like one of those nice public bathrooms that you see on TV, with attendants and breath mints and real monogrammed towels. It's a Burger King bathroom. And not a particularly clean one, either.

I take a wad of toilet paper off the roll and blow my nose loudly. The most disgusting part of this whole thing is that I'm sitting on the toilet while I do this. Because there's no top to the toilets. So I'm actually sitting on the toilet. Without my pants down, of course. Who knows what kind of disgusting germs are transferring themselves onto my skirt. I'm probably going to have to burn it after this. Which is horrible, because I've never even worn it before. In fact, the only reason I'm even wearing it now is because I wanted Jordan to think I was dressing up for Lloyd. Which is really screwed up. I don't know when I lost my sanity, but it's not a good feeling.

I throw the toilet paper with my snot on it into the toilet and flush. I just need to take a deep breath. The trip is half over. That should make me feel better, but really, it doesn't. It makes me feel worse, because the past couple of days have seemed like a lifetime.

I head out of the stall and start washing my hands at the sink. The bathroom is deserted, which is good because it would be embarrassing for someone to see me looking like this—eyes red from crying, ketchup stain on my cute new shirt, and my hair a mess from when I kept running my hands through it in the stall in an effort not to touch anything germ infested.

"Court?" Jordan's voice comes from outside the bathroom.

"What?" I say, trying to make it out like I didn't just go running from his car crying and into the bathroom.

"You okay?"

"Yeah," I say. "I'm fine."

"Okay," he says. There's a pause. "Was it . . . Are you upset about the food? We can go somewhere else?"

He thinks I started crying over fast-food burgers. He

can't be that stupid, can he? He obviously knows I'm upset about him, and he's just trying to be nice. Great, pity. Just what I need.

"No, the food was fine," I say. "I think I'm just a little upset about seeing Lloyd."

"Why would you be upset about that?" he asks, sounding confused. Good question.

"Not upset about seeing him," I say. I wet a paper towel and use it to wipe my face off. It feels scratchy and kind of gross, but I put up with the momentary discomfort so that I can look human again. "Upset because I haven't seen him for a while."

"You just saw him two days ago," he says.

I throw the paper towel away, pull my shirt down a little bit so that the ketchup stain is less noticeable, and emerge from the bathroom. He's leaning against the wall, his hair wet from the rain, and he looks really, really, cute. And really, really worried about me. I will NOT start crying again.

"Yeah, well, when you're in love with someone, two days can seem like an eternity." I toss my hair defiantly over my shoulder and start walking toward the door. My attempt at haughtiness is overshadowed by the fact that the shoes I'm wearing (cute sparkly purple flip-flops with butterflies on them) are drenched from the rain, and so every time I stomp, my shoes squish.

"So, wait, now you guys are in love?" Jordan asks, sounding confused.

"Yes," I say definitively. "And since you really care about your new girlfriend, I'm sure you understand how two days without seeing someone can really seem like a long time."

"Yeah," he says, not sounding sure. "But Court, I really doubt you're in love with Lloyd."

"Whatever, Jordan," I say. "Not to sound like a brat or anything, but you don't really know me anymore. I'm a new woman."

We're in the parking lot now, and I open the door to his TrailBlazer and pull myself into the passenger seat. He gets in and starts the car. I pull my seat belt on and decide it's time for a new attitude. No more crying.

"Let's go to Middleton," I say. "I can't freakin' wait to get there."

Jocelyn calls two hours later, while we're stuck in traffic. I'm looking through a magazine that I bought at a rest stop and reading an article about what to do if you get dumped. It's actually not helping me much, because I'm pretty sure it's satire. The article, not the magazine. It basically says that once a guy dumps you, you should cease worrying about what he thinks of you, and that you shouldn't try denying your psychotic urges, because it's not natural. It says that if you feel like you want to stalk him, you totally should. If you want to break into his email account, do it. Drive-bys? Harassing his new girlfriend? Totally allowed. It's quite scary, actually. The article, I mean.

I flip open my phone. "Whaddup?" I say, tossing my

magazine onto the floor. I'm totally over my nervous break-down. You'd think I'd feel good about this, but I don't. For some reason, it makes me uneasy, like the fact that I got over it so quickly just means that something worse is going to come. It's like I'm in some sort of denial mode.

"So he wasn't hanging out with Katelyn," Jocelyn says, sounding smug. Which makes no sense, because in order to sound smug, you have to be right about something. And since Jocelyn thought that B. J. was cheating on her, and now she's found out that he isn't, she shouldn't sound smug. She should sound sheepish.

"How do you know?" I ask.

"He caught me stalking him," she says breezily.

"He caught you?" I ask, wondering why she's not more upset. I feel Jordan shift in his seat next to me. I look at him suspiciously and when he catches my eye, he nervously adjusts the rearview mirror.

"Yes, he caught me." Jocelyn sighs. I hear the sound of splashing in the background, and music. Loud music.

"Where are you?" I ask.

"At a pool party," she says.

"Hold on," I say, pushing the volume up on my phone in an effort to hear her over the background noise. "How did you end up at a pool party?"

"Hailie Roseman invited me," she says simply. "So B. J. drove us here."

"No," I say. Is she drunk? "I mean, how did you get

from stalking B. J., to getting caught, to ending up at Hailie Roseman's pool party?" I don't even think Jocelyn is friends with Hailie Roseman, a junior who I always suspected Jordan of hooking up with, even though he constantly denies it.

"Oh," Jocelyn says. "That's actually why I'm calling." Duh. "See, B. J. found out I was stalking him because Jordan told him it was me."

"Oh, really?" I say. "He told him it was you?" Jordan shifts in his seat again, then reaches over and starts flipping through the satellite stations. He clears his throat.

"Yes," Jocelyn repeats. "Jordan told him."

"And how did Jordan know?"

"I guess he figured it out because you were telling him to tell B. J. not to call the police."

"Really," I say, contemplating this revelation.

"Mm-hmm," Jocelyn says. More splashing. "But listen, that's not the best part."

"What's the best part?" I ask, not really seeing what was so good about the first part. Jordan looks over at me curiously. Ha. Like I'm really going to clue him in on what's going on. I like making him squirm. Also, since the traffic isn't moving, it isn't really like he can do anything about the fact that I'm making him uncomfortable. He just has to sit there.

"So after B. J. caught me and I confessed, we had this really long talk," Jocelyn says. Her voice sounds kind of slurred, like she's been drinking. More splashing and music in the background. I love the fact that my friends are off having an end-of-summer party with drinks and swimming and music and I'm stuck on the road trip from hell. So not fair.

"That's great, Joce," I say, meaning it. "You and B. J. *should* be able to talk about things more openly. I think it'll really help you to feel more comfortable with the situation."

"So, listen," she says, sounding kind of nervous. "I have to tell you something that he told me. He told me so that I'd feel more like I could trust him."

"You mean like a secret?"

"Yeah," she says, sounding nervous again. "Exactly like a secret." I wrack my brain for what kind of secrets B. J. could possibly have. A criminal record? No, he wouldn't keep that a secret. When he burned our class year into the school lawn and almost didn't graduate, he bragged about it to anyone who would listen, including two girls he'd never met that happened to overhear us talking about it one night at a random ice cream stand. An STD? Nah, Jocelyn would be freaking out. And she doesn't sound freaked out.

"Okay," I say, wondering how she could possibly think it's a good idea to put a start to her new, trusting relationship with her boyfriend by telling me a secret he told her not to tell. But I don't tell her this, because I kind of want to know the secret.

"Now, I know it's probably not the best idea to tell you, you know, since we're now having an open, honest, communication based on mutual trust and respect," she says, sounding kind of like Dr. Phil. It's hard to take her seriously, though, because even though she's talking like she understands the psychobabble she's spewing, I can still hear the sounds of the party in the background, including a male voice that's yelling, "LET'S GET FUCKED UP!" over and over again. This is being met by cheers of "Woooo!"

"Then why are you?" I ask.

"Hold on," she says. "I'm going inside the house, it's getting loud out here."

"Okay," I agree. I roll down my window.

"What are you doing?" Jordan asks. "The AC is on."

"I want some air," I tell him.

"How can you possibly want some air?" he asks, frowning. "The AC is on. It's hotter outside than it is in here."

"I didn't say I was hot," I say. "I said I needed some air." The guy in the car next to us is apparently so fed up with the traffic that he's gotten out of his car and is rummaging around in his trunk. He emerges with what looks like travel Scrabble, and looking satisfied, slams his trunk shut.

"I can't believe we forgot to bring our travel games," Jordan says, I guess thinking he's funny.

"Hello!" I yell into the phone. No response. How long does it take to get into someone's house? I can still hear the sounds of the party in the background, so I know she didn't hang up. Maybe she dropped her phone. "Helllloo!" I yell again, thinking maybe she'll hear me and come back.

"Why are you yelling?" Jordan asks.

"Because Jocelyn put me on hold and she hasn't come back yet."

"Well, there's another person in this car. So try not to yell."

"Oh, I'm sorry," I say. "Is my yelling bothering you?"

"Well, yes," he says. "Besides, it's not like you're in a big rush to get her back on the phone, right? You're not doing anything important. We're sitting in traffic."

"Wow," I say. "You're so astute, Jordan. I love how totally insightful and good you are at reading situations."

He looks away then, and I yell, "HELLLOOO!" into the phone once more.

"Oh, hi," Jocelyn says, sounding breathless. "Sorry about that. I couldn't figure out how to open the back door, so I had to walk all the way around the house, and it took a while." I want to ask her why she didn't just talk to me while she walked, or at least pick up the phone to give me a status report, but I don't.

"Anyway," I say.

"Yeah, anyway, I'm inside now."

"Good."

"Yup."

"So . . ."

"Oh right! The secret. Okay, so I know I probably shouldn't be telling you."

"Probably not," I agree. "But before we get into it, who was that yelling 'Let's get fucked up!' like that over and over? Just out of curiosity, I mean."

"Oh, that was B. J.," she says. "He's getting drunk tonight." I think it's a great sign that they're celebrating their newfound, trusting relationship by getting drunk and blabbing each other's secrets, but I don't say this. I'm not one to pass judgment on anyone's relationships.

"Oh, okay."

"Anyway, I know I shouldn't tell you, but the reason I am is because it's kind of about you. Well, indirectly anyway. And I do want to be loyal to B. J., I really do, but you're my best friend, and if you found out from someone else, and then you found out I knew and didn't tell you, you'd probably be pissed. And chicks over dicks, you know?"

"Okay," I say, starting to get worried. I don't like Jocelyn finding secrets out that have to do with me from B. J., because inevitably they're going to involve Jordan. And the fact that I just had a breakdown in a public rest room makes me very nervous about my mental state.

"Okay," she says. "B. J. told me that Jordan made up the MySpace girl."

"What do you mean?" I ask. My heart is beating really fast all of a sudden, and I wonder if Jordan can hear it.

"The girl he supposedly met on MySpace? That he dumped you for? He didn't dump you for her. He made her up."

"Why would he do that?" I ask.

"I have no idea," she says, but even as she's saying it, I know the answer. He did it as an excuse to break up with me. He knew it would be easier if he had a reason, something concrete that would at least give me some sort of answer. And this whole time, I've been making myself feel better by thinking up horrible attributes to Jordan's new girlfriend, telling myself she's a slut, and someday he'll realize what a huge mistake he's made.

The truth is, he just doesn't love me.

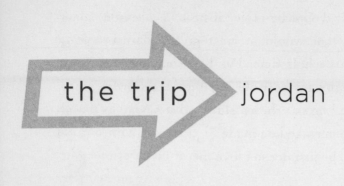

the trip jordan

Day Two, 5:06 p.m.

Courtney is making me extremely nervous. Whatever the fuck is going on in her phone conversation cannot be good. I've already figured out that she knows I tipped B. J. off to the whole Jocelyn thing, which makes me slightly annoyed. When I told him, it was so she wouldn't get in trouble, not so he could go and tell her how he found out. He had to know she was going to come back and tell Courtney. What was he thinking?

The traffic inches slowly forward, and Courtney sits next to me in silence. When we get to Middleton twenty minutes later, the vibe in the car is not any better. I wish Courtney would just talk to me and tell me how pissed off she is, but that's obviously not going to happen.

Add that to the fact that I have four missed calls on my phone, all from Courtney's dad, who I have most definitely decided is the craziest motherfucker that I know. Seriously, his shit is whacked. I used to think maybe B. J. was the craziest person I know, but now I realize that B. J. only does crazy things, and that there is a definite difference between acting crazy and being crazy. And Courtney's dad is the latter.

Since we've been stuck in traffic, and Courtney's been giving me the silent treatment, I've come up with a great plan for our time in North Carolina. It consists of one part: Stay away from Courtney and Lloyd, and hang out with my brother only. This is going to be slightly problematic, since I'm not sure how Courtney is going to feel about me just dropping her off at the gates of Middleton. If they even have gates.

I pull the car into the visitor parking lot and switch off the car. "Well," I say. "I guess this is it."

"What do you mean?" she asks, frowning.

"I mean, I guess this is it. This is where we part ways."

"Part ways?" she asks, and it could be my imagination, but for some reason she looks almost panicked.

"Yeah, you know," I say. "Part ways, leave each other, go in different directions."

"Why would we do that?" She bites her lip and looks out the car window.

"Why wouldn't we? I'm sure you want time alone with Lloyd, and really, I don't want to be around that shit." Whoops. Shouldn't have said that out loud. Last thing I need is for her thinking I want her back. Even though I do. Actually, not true. I never wanted to break up with her. But whatever. Semantics. "Lloyd and I aren't exactly BFFs, if you know what I mean."

She nods. She's probably thinking about the time Lloyd and I almost got into a fistfight.

"So!" I say cheerfully. I pull the keys out of the ignition. "I'll open the back so you can get your stuff."

"Great!" she says. She pulls out her cell phone and makes a big production of turning it on silent. I guess so her and Lloyd won't get interrupted while they're hooking up.

"Just make sure you close the truck when you're finished," I say. I grab my black duffle from the back and sling it over my shoulder.

"That's all you have?" she asks. "I mean, that's all your bringing? For the overnight."

"Yeah, that's all I'm bringing for the overnight," I say.

"Well, I have a lot more than you," she says pointedly. If she thinks I'm going to help her carry her stuff, she's definitely mistaken. I like to consider myself a nice guy, but I draw the line at helping my ex-girlfriend bring her stuff up to some guy's dorm room. That's insane. Especially since it's pretty obvious that she's planning on sleeping with him.

"Of course you have a lot more than me," I say. "You're a girl. But take your time getting whatever you need. Just make sure you close the back when you're done. I'll meet you here tomorrow at eight, and we'll get back on the road, all right?"

"Yeah, okay," she says, not sounding okay with it at all.

A look of hurt passes across her face briefly as I turn away, and it's almost enough to make me turn around, but then I think about Lloyd and the MySpace comment, and I keep on walking.

My brother, Adam, lives in a single room in Gluster Hall, where he's an RA. We're not super close, and I'm not sure why that is. I think it might have something to do with the fact that we were so spoiled growing up, that it made it easy not to have to interact. My parents bought us every- thing—video game systems, DVDs, cell phones, toys, whatever we wanted. Which means there wasn't a lot of time spent sitting around, reading books or hanging out, making forts and trying to amuse ourselves with imaginary games.

I knock on his door and he opens it wearing a pair of boxers and a T-shirt.

"Dude," Adam says, squinting at me. "Are you fucking kidding me?" If you knew my brother, you'd know this isn't really strange. He talks like this a lot, in random questions that make no sense. "Are you fucking kidding me?" is actu- ally one of his favorites.

"What's up, bro?" I ask, and contemplate pulling him into a hug. We're not usually very touchy-feely, but he is my brother and I haven't seen him in a while. Before I can decide if this would be appropriate, I catch a whiff of pot coming from his room. I look at him again. His eyes are bloodshot and he has a half-grin on his face. That's just great. The asshole is high.

"Dude, are you fucking kidding me? Right now?" he repeats.

"Uh, no," I say. "I guess not. But it's, uh, good to see you." I realize he's blocking the door, so I take a step closer to him, in an effort to show my intent to actually get into his room. Although I'm sure once I get in there, I'm going to start getting a pot buzz by default.

He still doesn't move out of the way, and I bump into him awkwardly. For the first time, I realize he's not wearing any shoes. I know this because I step on his foot.

"You're not coming in," he says, putting his hand up.

"What do you mean?" I ask, confused.

"Why didn't you tell me about Mom?" he asks, and I realize he's not only high but pissed. Psychotically, scary pissed. His eyes are rimmed in red out of anger, not just from pot. I thought pot was supposed to make you mellow.

"What do you mean, 'tell you about Mom?'" I ask, automatically reverting to avoid-and-deny mode.

"About Mom having an affair, about how she's leaving Dad for someone else," he says, and this time he bangs his fist against the door. I take a step back.

"I didn't know," I say quietly, which is only a half lie. I knew she was having an affair, but I didn't know she was going to leave my dad. Suddenly, I feel like someone's punched me in the stomach.

"That's bullshit," he says, leaning against the door frame. "That's bullshit and you know it. She told me you knew. She told me you caught them."

"I did," I say, "But I didn't know she was going to leave Dad because of it. She acted like it wasn't a big deal, like it was a random thing that was going to stop." In reality, I knew this wasn't true. My mom had said that to me, but it was pretty obvious that's not what was going on. I figured maybe she just needed time to end it—I mean, let's face it. Courtney's dad is one fucked-up motherfucker. I didn't know exactly what was going on, but I knew there was a chance he could have been making it difficult for my mom the way he was making my life difficult.

"So that made it okay not to tell me? Jesus, Jordan!" He runs his fingers through his hair and looks at me like he can't believe my obvious stupidity.

"It wasn't mine to tell," I say. "It was up to her to tell Dad, it wasn't my place."

"You're right," he says. "At first. But this shit has been going on for months, Jordan. Were you ever going to tell anyone?" Suddenly, he seems very coherent and not like he's been smoking pot at all, which scares me. My brother is quite a bit bigger than me, but it's not like I think he wants to fight me. We've been in fistfights before. Nothing major, just little scrapes that started out over something dumb and then escalated to the point where we would rough each other up a bit. But now, he doesn't even seem like his words are motivated by anger. It's something else — almost like a hatred.

"I don't know if I was going to tell anyone," I say.

"That's great," Adam says and then slams the door in my face. I stand there for a minute, staring at the door and trying to calm down. Then I pick up my stuff and head back out to my car. When I get there, Courtney and her bags are gone.

courtney ▸ the trip

Day Two, 5:19 p.m.

I can do this. I can pretend I like Lloyd. I've been in school plays before. Well, not since junior high, and even then it was just a bit part that was akin to being in the chorus. I didn't have any actual lines or anything. But still. I had to act through my facial expressions.

I've been standing outside Lloyd's dorm for about ten minutes, my pink duffle bag slung over my shoulder and my cell phone in my hand. I want to call him, really I do, but for some reason, I can't. Technically, I can't get into the building unless he comes down to get me, since they have some sort of swipe card system to get in the dorms. I guess it's for security reasons, although there have already been two helpful students who have offered to swipe me in. So much for secure dorms.

"Courtney?" I turn around and there's Lloyd, standing behind me.

"Oh!" I say. "Hi! I was just about to call you." I hold up my cell phone, to prove my point. It's not like I'm lying. I really was about to call him. Or at least, I was about to *try* to call him. And effort should count for something.

"I came down, just in case you couldn't find the dorm." He wraps his arms around me and I lean into his body. "I'm so glad you're here," he murmurs into my hair. I bury my face into his neck and try to make myself feel something, anything for him. I wrack my brain for all the things I loved about him while I lusted after him for the past six years. His arms, which I always thought were really buff, now just feel . . . I don't know, hard. Okay, not the arms, not the arms. Hmm. I used to spend a lot of time thinking about kissing him. But now that I've actually kissed him, I can't really think about what it would be like anymore, because I've already done that. And it wasn't bad exactly, but it wasn't great either. Nothing like kissing Jordan.

"I'm glad I'm here, too," I say, sort of meaning it. I don't know what's going to happen with Lloyd and I, but being out of that car can only be a good thing.

"Let's get your stuff inside," Lloyd says. He takes my pink duffle bag, and I follow him into the dorm.

Two hours later, I feel like I might want to kill myself. It all started when I got a glimpse of Lloyd's closet. For some weird reason, Lloyd must have decided that when he unpacked all his stuff, it would be a good idea to start with his clothes. Actually, not all his clothes, but just his polo shirts. So now his room is pretty bare, but his closet, which is open, has all these polo shirts hanging in it. For some reason, this seems weird to me. I keep thinking about this one time when Jordan called Lloyd "Polo Boy" by accident in front of me.

I was on the phone with Jordan, and I clicked over to the other line, and when I came back, Jordan was like, "Was that Polo Boy?"

And I was all, "Who?"

And Jordan was like, "Nothing."

Apparently he and B. J. call Lloyd "Polo Boy" and he accidentally let it slip. He thought I'd be pissed, but I wasn't. At the time, I actually found it really, really funny. But now, looking at all the shirts hanging up in Lloyd's closet, something about it is kind of . . . disturbing. Does he not like any other shirts? Does he even have any other shirts? I think I saw him in a T-shirt once. When we were in the same gym class.

"So I see you unpacked all your clothes," I say, running my hands down the line of shirts in the closet.

"Yup," he says. He's sitting on the bed, and I know I'm supposed to probably go sit down next to him, but I'm afraid if I do, he might start trying to kiss me or something, and I really, really don't want that to happen. I'm hoping that maybe if I hang out with him a little longer, I'll start feeling more comfortable. This is, after all, the very first time we've hung out since we hooked up. And hooking up with him couldn't have been that bad. I mean, it went on for a while. We were making out for at least an hour or two, and I can't see myself doing that if it was really, really bad.

"Cool," I say. For some reason, I can't stop looking at his shirts. Or touching them. I'm, like, stroking his shirts right now. Over and over, like some sort of shirt pervert.

"Come sit down," Lloyd says, patting the spot on the bed next to him.

"Okay," I say uncertainly. I sit down next to him.

"So what do you want to do tonight?' He takes my hand in his, and interlaces his fingers with mine. I don't know what to do. I have no plan. I figured Jordan would be hanging out with us, at least for a little while, and that I would have to pretend to be interested in Lloyd when I really wasn't. But now, I realize that was the most ridiculous thing I've ever thought in my life. Jordan and Lloyd don't like each other. Why would we all hang out?

"Uh, I don't know," I say, looking around the room. I realize I'm supposed to sleep here tonight, and suddenly, I feel like I'm going to throw up.

"Maybe just hang out here," Lloyd says. His index finger is now making circles on the back of my hand. I try to slide out of his grip without him noticing, but I think he thinks I'm stroking his hand, because he grabs it. Hard. Normally, I like a guy who knows what he's doing, but this feels, um, kind of weird.

"Or maybe we could go somewhere," I say. "Like to a movie." Actually, wait, bad idea. Visions of dark movie theaters and Lloyd rubbing my hand definitely does not make me feel comfortable.

"A movie sounds good," he says. His mouth is against my neck now, and I can feel his breath while he's talking. Which you think would feel good, but for some reason, I'm now thinking of Lloyd as being Polo Boy, defined only by his polo shirts, and therefore, his breath has now become polo breath. I am definitely about to have another breakdown.

"Or!" I say. "You could show me the campus." A walking tour sounds good. A walking tour sounds very safe, something high school kids do with their parents. Something that we'd have to be standing up to do. Although I suppose people do kiss and make out (and have sex?) standing up. But it would be in public. So it would be limited.

"You really want to see the campus right now?" Lloyd asks. He turns my head toward his and kisses me. He's kissing me. Right now, his tongue is in my mouth. I'm kissing him back. It doesn't feel horrible, but it doesn't feel right either. It's like we have no kissing chemistry or something.

"Lloyd," I say, breaking away. "I think we should go somewhere, I mean, we have the whole night to . . ." I'm trying to figure out a way to say "hook up" without actually saying "hook up" when I suddenly realize that I don't have to hook up with him. Jordan is gone. I don't have to pretend to want to hook up with Lloyd.

"I'm sorry," Lloyd says, talking into my neck. "I don't want you to think I just want to mess around."

"Oh, that's okay," I say. In a way, it actually might be better if he does just want to hook up. Because then, when I tell him it can't happen, he won't be that upset. It won't be like there are feelings involved or anything. He'll just be like, "Oh, okay, I'll just find some other girl to hook up with. La, la, la." And then we can go back to being friends. Friends that have kissed. And made out a little. And then visited each other at college, where someone decided they didn't want to hook up anymore. Hmmm.

"Because I really do like you, Courtney," he says. "I never told you this, but when you were with Jordan, it made me realize that I've had feelings for you all this time."

"Oh." Great. I look at Lloyd, and suddenly, I feel like a horrible person. What am I doing? Messing with my best friend's head so that I can make some guy who made up a fake girlfriend jealous? That's completely and totally insane. It's like I don't even realize who I am anymore.

"Lloyd, listen," I say. "I can't stay here."

"What do you mean?" he asks, looking confused. He takes my hand again.

"I just can't stay here," I repeat. I feel like I'm suffocating. I'm thinking about Jordan making up the MySpace girl, and being here with Lloyd, and I just can't take it. I need to get out of there. Immediately.

"What are you talking about?" he says.

"This," I say, gesturing. "I just . . . I can't. I'll call you later." I pick up my bag, sling it over my shoulder. I need to get outside. Fast.

Lloyd calls after me, but I ignore it, and once I get outside, I feel much better. I take a deep breath. That was the right thing to do. I couldn't stay there, especially after he told me that he liked me. That would have been cruel. And horrible. But now I realize I have no plan. I don't know where to go, where to stay, or what to do. I head back to Jordan's car, figuring at least that's sort of a central location. And maybe he'll be hanging out there for some reason, and I'll just be able to weasel my way into spending the night in his brother's room.

But when I get to where Jordan's car was parked, he's not there. And his car is gone.

the trip ⟩ jordan

Day Two, 6:43 p.m.

I'm sitting in a motel down the street from Middleton contemplating my life when my cell phone rings. It's B. J., and I want to ignore it, but from what I could tell, he was at some party and he might need help. Not that there's anything much I can do from North Carolina, but still. He could have alcohol poisoning or something. Plus, if he's not in any kind of trouble, I'm going to bitch him out for telling Jocelyn I told him she was the one following him. How is it that I am away from home, and yet I still have all this drama? I've spent the past half an hour on the computer in the lobby, on Courtney's MySpace page, reading the comment Lloyd left her, and then scrolling back through ALL her comments, trying to find some clue of exactly what happened. Did they have sex? I checked his page, too, but she hasn't left any comments for him since they hooked up. Although ominously enough, he's changed his "relationship status" from "single" to "in a relationship," which is slightly suspect. The information age is so psychotic—without the cell phone and Internet, I would be drama free right now.

"Yeah," I say into the phone, hoping my tone conveys the idea that I'm pissed, but will still help him if he's dying.

"'Sup, kid?" B. J. asks. He doesn't sound like he's alcohol poisoned. I kick my shoes off and sit down on the hotel room bed. I hate hotel rooms. There's something unreal about them, and temporary, like you're on borrowed time or something.

"Nothing," I say, making sure to keep it short.

"Listen," B. J. says. "I'm drunk."

"Okay." He's talking, which means he can't be too drunk. So he's probably calling to apologize. I'm upset that he didn't call until he was shit-faced, but I guess a drunken apology is better than no apology at all.

"I have to tell you something," B. J. says, sounding nervous. I consider telling him I already know, but then decide it's more fun to make him squirm for a while.

"Oh, yeah? What's that?" I pick up the remote and turn on the TV. That's another thing about hotel rooms. You have to pay ten dollars to order movies. Movies should come with your hotel room. It should be a perk, like the pool.

"First, let me just say that I'm really, really sorry," B. J. says.

"Mm-hmm," I say. I flip through the channels, wondering if the Devil Rays game will be on TV in North Carolina.

I turn to ESPN, but for some reason, they're showing the Cardinals game, which makes no sense, since the Cardinals play in St. Louis, and Tampa is much closer to North Carolina than St. Louis is. I wait for the little bar at the bottom of the screen to show the game update.

"And I want you to know that I wasn't thinking when I did it. It's just that Jocelyn really had me by the balls."

"Okay," I say, sighing. Tampa's losing 4–0 to the Yankees. Fucking Yankees. I'm actually glad that the game isn't being shown now, because if I was watching it, I'd get pissed.

"So," B. J. says. "Uh, the thing is, that I kind of told Jocelyn about the MySpace girl." Pause. "But don't worry, she's not going to tell anyone," he adds quickly.

"You told her what about the MySpace girl?" I ask, sighing. This MySpace girl is really starting to become a pain in my ass. It's impossible to remember what I've told people about her. It wasn't as simple as just telling Courtney I had a new girlfriend. I had to tell other people as well, to get the word out. In fact, the only one who knows the truth about the whole thing is B. J. I didn't plan the MySpace girl well enough—I should have written down all her vital stats, so that I could keep track of who I told what to. I wonder if I should stage a MySpace breakup.

"I told Jocelyn about her," B. J. repeats.

"Yes, B. J.," I say, forcing myself to keep my patience because I know he's drunk. "But what did you tell Jocelyn about the MySpace girl?" Fifty bucks says whatever he told Jocelyn, Courtney already knows. Those two tell each other everything.

"I told her the truth about her. About how you made her up." I'm sure I've misheard him.

"I'm sure I've misheard you," I say, muting the television. B. J. is not that stupid. He wouldn't do something so ridiculously stupid. Would he? I think about all the stupid things B. J. has done in the past, and suddenly, I feel sick.

"Now, don't start freaking out," B. J. says, sounding nervous again, because I'm sure I sound like I'm about to flip the fuck out. "Jocelyn said she wasn't going to tell Courtney."

"And you believed her?" I ask incredulously. "Are you fucking kidding me right now?" I add, borrowing a line from my brother. "They tell each other everything! Every single thing! Courtney probably knows how big your dick is!"

B. J. gasps. I'm not sure if it's because I'm yelling or because Courtney might know how big his dick is. Probably a little bit of both.

"I can't believe you told her!" Suddenly, I'm irate. This uncontrollable anger is coming over me, and I think it's everything—the whole situation with my parents, my brother kicking me out of his dorm, being in this fucking hotel room when the Devil Rays are losing to the Yankees, the whole situation with Courtney and the MySpace girl . . . I'm pissed off. More pissed than I've ever been in my life.

And at that moment, Courtney's dad decides to beep in on my call waiting.

"What!" I say when I get to the other line. I don't even bother telling B. J. to hold on. Either he'll figure it out or think I hung up on him. Either way is fine with me.

"Hey," Frank says. He always acts like we're the best of friends, which could quite possibly be the most annoying thing about him.

"What do you want?"

"I just wanted to check in, see how the trip is going," he says. "I tried Courtney's cell phone, but she's not answering it."

"It's over," I say, not realizing I mean it until the words are out of my mouth.

"What is?" he asks, sounding confused.

"I'm telling her the truth." And with that, I hang up on both B. J. and Courtney's dad, shut my cell phone off, and head out of the motel to find Courtney.

courtney | the trip ⇒

Day Two, 7:19 p.m.

I don't know what else to do, so I head over to Jordan's brother Adam's dorm. Maybe I could tell them Lloyd and I are fighting? Or that he proposed to me, and when I said I wasn't ready to get married, he kicked me out of the room. Hmm. It's going to be challenging, trying to come up with an explanation that makes sense as to why I have nowhere to sleep tonight.

Adam's building has the same swipe card system as Lloyd's did, but for some reason, there are no people coming in and out. Maybe Lloyd's building is like, the party building, where people are just coming and going all the time. And Adam's building is the studious building, and all the kids are in their rooms studying.

A girl in a pink tank top and tons of eyeliner walks up the steps, and I try to follow her into the building, but she turns around and gives me a death glare. I am a master at the death glare (I perfected it even more just for this trip), but this girl is really, really good.

"You can't come in without your card," she says.

"I forgot my card," I say.

"You forgot it?" She tosses her hair over her shoulder.

"Yeah," I say. "I forgot it in my room."

"Not my problem," she says and starts shutting the door. "Go to the student center and get a temporary." And then she shuts the door in my face. God, I hope she's not leading the prospective student tours around this place. Who would want to go to school here? So far, I know three people here. Lloyd, Adam, and Pink Shirt. Lloyd is currently pissed off at me because I won't hook up with him, Pink Shirt was just a bitch to me, and one time, Jordan's brother told him he should break up with me because I had no tits. This place is so great.

I pull out my cell phone, which for some reason is on silent. Oh. From when I made that big show about putting it on silent when Jordan dropped me off here. So that Lloyd and I could hook up. I take a deep breath and con-template what I'm going to say. Something to make it look like I ditched Lloyd? But then I realize that this whole time, this whole game I've been playing about the Lloyd thing is kind of pointless. Because I was hoping to make Jordan jealous by using Lloyd to make him come to his senses — i.e., realize MySpace Mercedes was a total slut, while I, on the other hand, was so obviously desired and cool that I was moving on at the speed of light. But now that I know the MySpace girl is made up, it kind of ruins it. He just doesn't like me. Or love me. So it doesn't matter if I have a boyfriend or not, because he doesn't care.

I feel like I'm going to cry, so instead of calling Jordan, I follow the signs to the student union and order a pink lemonade, which I drink while sitting on a bench outside and trying to figure out how long I have until it gets really dark and I'm forced to do something. My cell phone rings. It's my dad.

"Hey," I say, trying to sound like everything's fine. Must not sound like I am stuck with no place to spend the night after getting attacked in Lloyd's dorm room. Okay, not really attacked. More like accosted. But still. I can't let my dad know I have nowhere to sleep.

"Hey, honey," he says, and something in his voice makes me nervous.

"What's wrong?" I ask.

"Listen, Courtney," he says. "I have something that I need to tell you."

before ◀ jordan

17 Days Before the Trip, 6:23 p.m.

"I'm breaking up with her tonight," I tell B. J. We're on the phone, and I'm waiting for Courtney to come over to my house. "I can't keep doing this. It's ridiculous."

"Okay," B. J. says uncertainly. "But I don't understand why you can't just tell her."

"I could just tell her," I say. "But the thing is, B. J., what if she's never supposed to find out? What if this thing with her dad and my mom runs its course, and what she doesn't know isn't going to hurt her unless I tell her?"

"Well," B. J. says, "if she's never going to find out, then why would you break up with her? It's not going to hurt anyone. Especially if she's going to start giving it up. Don't give up a piece of ass just to spite your face." He sounds smug.

"I'm not even going to address that," I say, leaning back in my chair and running my fingers through my hair. "This is going to be bad."

"Damn straight," B. J. says. "I hope she doesn't go psycho."

"Thanks," I say sarcastically. "You're such a good friend."

"Hey, I'm here for you, bro," he says. "But I think you're making a mistake."

"She loves me," I say. "And I can't be with someone who loves me when I'm lying to her. I'd rather have her hate me for thinking I'm a typical male asshole than by keeping something so important from her."

"Does she know it's going to happen?" B. J. asks.

"I told her we needed to talk tonight," I say, swallowing around the lump in my throat. "So I think so."

"You're a better man than I am, dude," B. J. says. "And may the force be with you." He clicks off, and I stare at my phone incredulously, partly because the fact that my conversation with B. J. is over means I'm going to have to deal with this whole Courtney thing, and partly because my best friend is quoting *Star Wars* when I'm in the middle of the biggest romantic crisis of my life.

Five minutes later, Courtney knocks on the door to my room. "Come in," I say, putting up an away message on my instant messenger that simply says "Away."

"Hey," she says. She's wearing a pair of red-and-white-checked shorts and a strappy red tank top. I can see the straps of her bra peeking through, and her hair is up in one of those sloppy ponytail/bun things girls always wear. She looks sexy.

"Hi," I say, not moving from my computer chair. She sits down on my bed and looks at me expectantly. Things with Courtney and I have not been the same since we got back from Miami. I've been slightly avoidant of her, and she's been standoffish with me, too. Once I didn't say "I love you" back to her, and once she made it clear she was ready to sleep with me and I didn't act on it, it's been awkward between us.

"Listen," she says. "I don't know what's going on with us, but I'm starting to feel really horrible about it." She bites her lip, and I look away from her. If I have to look at her, I'm not going to be able to do this. And it needs to be done.

"I don't want you to feel horrible, Court," I say truthfully. "And I don't want things to be weird between us."

"I'm sorry about Miami," she says. "I shouldn't have put pressure on you to have sex with me, and I shouldn't have told you I love you. I'm just . . . I just . . . I just got caught up in the moment, and I'm sorry."

I want so badly to take her in my arms and tell her it's okay, that I love her, too, but I can't. I look away, and don't say anything.

"But it doesn't have to change anything," she rushes on. "It's not a big deal. I mean, I don't need you to feel that way about me. Everything can go back to the way it was before, it doesn't have to be different. It doesn't have to change."

"It does change things, though, Courtney," I say, still not looking at her. "It does."

"It only does if we decide it does," she says. A note of worry has crept into her voice, like she knows this is something that can't be fixed, but it's for a different reason than she thinks, and it's killing me. "It doesn't matter to me, Jordan, really. I just want to go back to the way things were before."

"I can't," I say simply. "Courtney, on the beach I realized that I don't want to be tied down right now. I want to be able to be young and date other people." Oh, my God. I sound like a really old, annoying uncle who's trying to convince someone they should date while they can.

"You want to date other people?" she asks, her voice cracking a little bit.

"I'm not a relationship person," I say, shrugging. I still can't look at her, because I know if I do, I'll lose it.

There's a moment of silence, a pause, and I expect her to start screaming, or maybe to beg me to change my mind, or to start crying or something. But instead, she gets up from my bed and walks out my door. In a way, it's almost worse than a big scene. Because now she's probably never going to want to talk to me again. I wait until I hear the front door of my house shut before I give into it and start to cry.

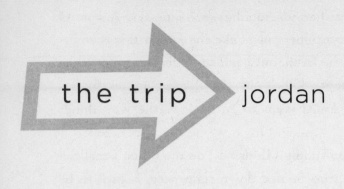

the trip > jordan

Day Two, 8:03 p.m.

"Where's Courtney?" I ask when Lloyd opens the door, not bothering with any pleasantries. I knew I was going to get into a fight with Lloyd at some point on this trip. It was inevitable. I thought maybe I'd be able to avoid it if I didn't see him, but now, when he answers the door to his room with a shit-eating grin on his face, I want to rip it off. His face, I mean.

"Well, well, well," Lloyd says, leaning against the door frame. "What's up, Jordy?" Lloyd is such a tool that he actually sometimes thinks he's cooler than me. Which is ridiculous. Especially since he's wearing a polo shirt. You cannot be cooler than anyone, especially not me, when you're wearing a polo shirt.

"Where's Courtney?" I repeat.

"Why?" he asks suspiciously, narrowing his eyes. "If you're here to do one of those last-minute things where you rush in and save her, you're a little too late." He smiles. He actually fucking smiles at me. I'm done with this dude.

I push him out of the way and walk right into his room. She's not there.

"She's not here," I say.

"Good work, Captain Obvious," he says. He crosses the room and sits down at his desk.

"Where. Is. She?" I ask. I wonder what will happen if I punch him. I'm so pissed off at everyone right now, the thought of getting into a fight with Lloyd actually scares me. I don't know if I could stop at just punching him. We'd probably get into it pretty good, and campus security would come and arrest me.

"I don't know," Lloyd says, shrugging. "I assume she's out looking for you."

"Why would she be out looking for me?"

"Because she left, and since she doesn't know anyone else here, I would assume she's looking for you," he says, rolling his eyes. Is this kid for real?

"You just let her leave?" I ask. "Why would you do that?"

"I don't know," he says. "She freaked out a little bit, and I figured she needed her space."

"You're an asshole," I say, pushing past him and outside. I pull my cell phone out of my pocket and dial her number, but she's not answering. Fuck. Where would she go? I head back toward the truck and dial her cell phone number on the way, hoping maybe she's turned it back on.

And then suddenly, I see her. She's sitting on a bench near where I parked my car. She's holding her cell phone in her hand, just looking at it. Which is weird, because I'm trying to call her. Her cell phone is ringing in her hand, and she's just ignoring it.

"Court!" I yell. I start walking toward her and she looks up. Her blue eyes meet mine, and suddenly, I stop. Because I can tell she knows.

"Hey," I say, walking toward her. She looks up, and the look she gives me is horrible. There are tears in her eyes. "Courtney," I say. "Let me explain."

"Let you explain?" She throws her head back and laughs at the absurdity of it. "Yeah, great, this should be interesting. Go ahead and explain."

"I didn't do it to lie to you," I say. "I wanted to protect you. I didn't know it was your dad, I didn't—"

"Great job of protecting me, Jordan," she says, cutting me off. "Do I look like you spared my feelings?" She picks up her bag and slings it over her shoulder, like she's going to leave. I reach up and grab her arm.

"Don't touch me!" she says, wrenching away from me.

"Court, please, listen—" I start to say.

"No," she says, standing up. "I'm done."

She starts walking away.

"Court!" I yell after her. "Where are you going?"

But she doesn't answer.

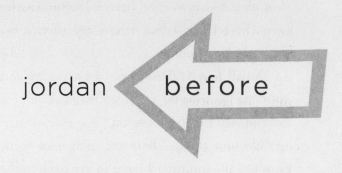

jordan before

13 Days Before the Trip, 3:30 p.m.

I'm walking out of the mall when I see Courtney's dad walking in. I try to get out of the way to avoid him, but he's already seen me, and I don't want to give him the satisfaction of seeing me turn around.

"Mr. Brewster!" I say cheerfully.

"Jordan," he says, nodding at me. "Looks like you've had a successful trip to the mall." The way he says it implies I've been on a silly little shopping trip, while he's been hard at work all day. Which is probably true. I've been in Abercrombie for more than an hour, and I've spent over four hundred dollars. All on my mom's credit card. Serves her right.

"I *have* had a successful trip," I agree.

"Abercrombie," he says, reading it off the bag in the same tone he used before. Sue me if I need retail therapy. This whole Courtney breakup is driving me insane, and shopping makes me feel better. I'm turning into a girl. Plus I love the feeling I get when my mom's credit card runs through the machine.

"Yup," I say. "You look like you could use a trip there yourself." It's meant to be an insult, like he has no sense of fashion, but he doesn't get it.

"Oh, not today," he says. "I'm here to upgrade my cell phone plan, and then I have to get back to the office."

"Good for you," I say, resisting the urge to hit him. "Good luck with that." I move past him into the parking lot, but he calls after me.

"I heard you and Courtney broke up," he says. "I'm sorry to hear that."

"I'm sure you are," I say sarcastically.

"Now, Jordan, that's not fair. I never wanted to cause you or Courtney any pain."

"It's not a big deal," I lie. "Courtney and I didn't break up because of you. We broke up because I met someone else." The last thing I want is to give Courtney's dad the satisfaction of thinking he broke the two of us up. Besides, this whole breakup with Courtney has spun out of control—I've made up a new girlfriend. A fake girlfriend, someone I supposedly met on MySpace. I got sick of everyone asking why we broke up, and I figured having a fake girlfriend is a better reason than "I don't know." Plus, it helps me when I get tempted to call Courtney and beg her to take me back.

"Well, that's great," Mr. Brewster says. He looks at his

watch and glances over my shoulder into the mall. "I should get going."

"Sure," I say. Asshole.

"I hope it won't be that big of a deal to you to drive to school without Courtney. Perhaps your new girlfriend could make the trip with you? It's an awful long way to go alone."

"What do you mean?" I ask, frowning. Court and I had planned to drive up to Boston together for school, and I figured it was still on. Actually, that's not true. I was hoping it was still on, but I was afraid to approach her about it since a) she won't talk to me, and b) if I brought it up, she might tell me it's canceled.

"Well, I assumed you wouldn't still be going on the trip. I haven't talked to Courtney about it yet, but —"

"Oh, no," I say. "We're still going."

"Really?" His eyebrows shoot up in surprise. "Does Courtney know this?"

"I haven't talked to her," I say. "But we're going." Suddenly I realize just how badly I want to go on this trip. That it could be my last chance to spend time with Courtney. And that since it's already planned, it won't look that suspicious if we still go.

"Jordan, I'm not sure that's the best idea," he says. "Courtney's already going through a lot with the breakup and —"

"We're going," I say. "You'll tell her she's still going. And if you don't, well . . ." I trail off, and I see a flash of panic cross his face. Because now that Courtney and I are broken up, he has no power over me. I could tell her everything if I wanted to. And with that, I turn around, head to my car, and drive home with my four hundred dollars' worth of Abercrombie merchandise in the trunk and the Beastie Boys on the radio.

courtney ← before

13 Days Before the Trip, 6:00 p.m.

"They're fucking making me go!" I scream into the phone. As a rule, I don't usually say the f-word, but this definitely warrants it.

"Um, okay," Jocelyn says, sounding confused. "You want to back up a little bit?"

"No, not really," I say. I throw myself down on my bed and reach over and crank up the AC that's in my window. I like my room frigid. My parents are always complaining about the electricity bill, but whatever. If they're going to make me suffer, I can totally make them suffer right back.

"Then I can't help you," Jocelyn says simply. I hear voices in the background.

"Where are you?" I ask.

"At the beach," she says. "With B. J. You wanna come down?"

"No thank you," I say. Why, why, why would my parents

do something like this? Why would they make me still go on this trip? I can kind of understand it from my mom, but my dad? He hates Jordan! I even offered to pay for the plane ticket myself, out of my graduation money, but nooo. The irony of all this is that B. J. and Jocelyn, who should be the poster children for dysfunctional relationships, are going strong. They're hanging out, cuddling, probably having sex on a beach, while Jordan and I, who NEVER EVEN FOUGHT, are done.

"So what are your parents making you do?" Jocelyn asks.

"They're making me go on the trip with Jordan! They said it's too late to get a ticket, and that I need to learn to take responsibility for my actions, and since I planned this trip, I should go." Saying the words out loud makes me so mad that I start punching the up button on the air conditioner, even though it's already as high as it can go.

"Are you serious?" Jocelyn says. "Courtney, I'm so sorry."

"We'll probably end up killing each other," I say, still hitting the air conditioner. Bang. Bang. My finger is starting to get a little sore, but for some reason, it's making me feel better. Maybe just because no more cool air is coming out doesn't mean the power isn't going up, therefore making the electricity bill get higher, therefore screwing my parents over.

"Yeah," Jocelyn says. "You probably will."

"Thanks a lot," I say. "I can't believe they would do

something like this to me. I'm only seventeen! Since when am I supposed to take responsibility for my actions?"

"I dunno," Jocelyn says. "It sucks, but hey, you'll probably learn a lot."

"Learn a lot!" I shriek, abandoning the air conditioner and burying my head in my pillow. "Don't get all deep on me now, Jocelyn."

"I'm just saying," she says. "Usually the hard stuff you're forced to do makes you learn a lot."

"I don't want to learn a lot," I say. "I already know enough."

"Sometimes you don't have a choice," Jocelyn says, and there's something in her tone of voice that makes me uncomfortable.

the trip > courtney

Day Two, 8:45 p.m.

I have never been so pissed off in my life. My heart is pumping at three million beats a second, and I'm consumed with rage.

And right now, I'm taking it out on the guy at the front desk of the Bellevue Motel who's trying to tell me you can't check in unless you have I.D. stating you're eighteen.

"But I just told you," I say, trying to keep my voice calm. "My I.D. was stolen. All I have is the cash I just happen to have in my pocket, which I can use to pay for the room." I wave around the emergency money my dad gave me just in case something went wrong on the trip. If this doesn't constitute something going wrong, I don't know what does.

"I understand that, ma'am," he says. "But it's motel policy."

"Well, that's just great!" I screech like some kind of crazy person. "I'll just sleep outside then, while I wait for my family to come get me. And while I'm out there, I'll call up some local newspeople and tell them what kind of establishment you're running here." I glance at his name tag. "Sound good, Scott?"

He looks nervous for a second, probably not because of my threat to call the media, but because I think he's getting the idea that I might be a bit unstable. He probably thinks I'm about two seconds away from coming back here and blowing the place up. "Let me see if there's any way the computer can circumvent the I.D. check," he says, tapping some buttons. Five minutes later, I'm on my way up to room 205.

I hate my dad, I hate Jordan, I even hate myself, because Jocelyn warned me he was bad news. I *knew* he was bad news. And I did it anyway. Which is so not like me. I don't get caught up in the moment. I analyze everything to death. I play it safe. And the first time I take a risk, look what happens. I end up wandering around a college campus in North Carolina, brokenhearted and with nowhere to go.

I pull out my cell phone and delete past the screen that says I have eighteen missed calls. Most of them are from my dad, who I hung up on when he told me he'd been cheating on my mom for the past six months.

"I have something to tell you, Courtney," he'd said, and I'd sat down on the bench, thinking maybe he was going to tell me he was sick, or my mom was sick, or that something bad happened to my grandma. Because he had that tone in his voice, the tone people get when they know they have to tell you something bad and they're dreading it.

"What is it?" I said, my heart in my stomach and my stomach in my throat.

"I'm having an affair," he'd said, and for a brief second, I thought he meant he was throwing a party or something. Like those people on that MTV show *My Super Sweet 16*. They're always referring to birthday parties as affairs. So I thought maybe my dad was planning a party, or that maybe he was even throwing one for me. But then I remembered that I'd already had a graduation party, a pretty big one actually, and that if my dad was going to throw a party, he definitely wouldn't sound so serious.

"An affair?" I asked.

"Yes," he said. "I've been cheating on your mother for the past six months." I couldn't believe the way he was saying it — it almost seemed kind of like a joke. He was using such horrible words. "Affair." "Cheat." It was like if it had been true, he would have tried to soften the blow a little bit.

"Okay," I said, not sure what I was supposed to do with this information.

"I'm so sorry to be telling you this now," he said, sounding like he meant it. "I didn't want to have to burden you with this while you're getting ready to start school." He sighed. "I know it's the last thing you should have to deal with, and I'm sorry for that, Courtney."

"Why are you telling me now?" I asked.

"Because Jordan said he was going to tell you if I didn't," he said. "And I knew you had to hear it from me." My heart skipped in my chest.

"How does Jordan know about it?" I asked, wondering when Jordan would have heard such a thing. How had he found out about this? We'd been on this trip for the past couple of days. Had he gotten a phone call from someone who found out?

"Jordan's known for a while, Courtney," my dad said. "He caught me with his mom a few months ago."

"You're having an affair with Jordan's mom?" I'm surprised, because Jordan's mom is so . . . I don't know. She's like this high-powered lawyer, totally the opposite of my mom, who's more glam. But maybe that's the problem.

"Yes," my dad said, sighing. And then I hang up the phone. On my dad. I hit the red button on my phone, like I'd just had a normal conversation that ended with "See you soon, love ya!" or some other pleasant sign-off.

Have I mentioned I'm pissed? I'm pissed at my dad, for thinking he could keep something like this from us. I'm angry that he thought I couldn't handle it, that he thought I would fall apart. I'm pissed that he was so selfish that he felt the need to keep things from me, just so he wouldn't have to deal with me being pissed off or upset. But most of all, I'm mad at Jordan. I'm mad that he didn't tell me what he knew, that he never felt he could be completely honest with me. I'm mad that he felt he needed to protect me, when I never gave him any indication I was weak.

I feel like I'm on that reality show *Joe Schmo*, where it turned out all the participants except one were paid actors. I feel like Joe Schmo. Courtney Schmo, whom everyone is lying to. I take a shower and change into my pajamas, then spend the next seven hours in my hotel room, watching celebrity countdowns on E! I'm starting to feel a little better, except for a moment during the countdown for the twenty-five hottest blondes, when I realize that some of the people featured on the countdown aren't natural blondes. Which feels like they're cheating. And being LIARS. CHEATING, LYING, BLONDES.

At four in the morning, I call Jordan's phone.

"Hello?" he says, sounding wide awake. I hear the sound of the TV in the background, so I know he's not sleeping in his car. I try to think of the worst place possible that would have a TV. Jail? A serial killer's basement? I try to wish him there.

"Oh, hello," I say, as if it's perfectly normal for me to be calling him at four in the morning.

"I've been trying to call you," he says. I've just turned my phone on, and as he's saying it, I hear the notification of my missed calls beeping in my ear. Fifty-six missed calls from Jordan. Ten from my dad. Six from Jocelyn. None from Lloyd. What an asshole. Although I'm not sure what's worse. Not calling at all, or calling fifty-six times.

"Really?" I say. "I must not have heard my phone."

"Courtney, where are you? Let me come and get you. We need to talk about this."

"I'm not telling you, and we don't need to talk about it," I say, trying to sound like a bitch. "I was just calling to make sure you still plan on driving the rest of the way to school with me tomorrow." I've thought about this a little bit, and I've decided I have two options:

1. Drive to school with Jordan, getting there on time. Once at school, follow previous plan of ignoring him and meeting fabulous college boyfriend.

2. Don't tell Jordan where I am, and find other way from North Carolina to Boston, which would most likely entail calling my dad to find out how I can get a plane ticket or a train or something. This actually might not be that bad, except I have a bad feeling my dad might hightail it to North Carolina and insist on escorting me to Boston himself. Either way, I would be late to school. And I have not gone through all of this to be late to orientation.

"Courtney, stop," Jordan says. "You're acting like a crazy person. Now tell me where you are, I'll come and get you, and we can talk. We can even start driving again, if you want."

"I'm not acting like a crazy person," I say, even though I totally am. Although I guess it's all relative. Finding out your dad is cheating on your mom with your ex-boyfriend's mother, and that your ex-boyfriend knew about it and didn't want to tell you so bad that he made up a MySpace girl is pretty traumatic. So calling someone at four in the morning probably isn't the worst thing I could be doing to deal with it. "And besides," I say. "Why would we start driving at four in the morning?" Jordan's driving is questionable at best on a good day, one where the sun is shining and there's no traffic.

"Because I know you're worried about getting there on time," he says, sounding like it's obvious.

"We're still going to get there on time," I say, a panicky feeling starting in my stomach. "We only have twelve hours to go."

"I know," he agrees. "We will still get there on time, but I just thought it might make you feel better if we left now. Since we're behind schedule."

"But we're not behind schedule," I say, exasperated. "We planned on staying in North Carolina until tomorrow." I glance at the clock. "Well, technically today, since it's four in the morning."

"Oh," he says.

"Which you would have known if you'd read the damn itinerary I gave you."

"I lost it," he says.

"Of course you did," I say.

"What's that supposed to mean?"

"Just what I said! That I'm not surprised you lost the itinerary, since you had no interest in any kind of schedule for this trip!"

"Well, maybe now I do," he says, sounding indignant.

"Maybe now you do what?" I ask. He's watching ESPN in the background. I can hear the SportsCenter music through the phone. I wonder if serial killers have cable. Probably. Lots of serial killers are totally normal people, with jobs and friends and all the pay channels.

"Maybe now I care about the schedule for the trip," he says, his voice sounding firm.

"Well, whatever," I say breezily. "Listen, I didn't call to fight with you." Which is kind of a lie. I did kind of call to fight with him. Or at least to wake him up, which obviously didn't work, since he was up at four in the morning like some kind of psychopath. Although I'm up at four in the morning as well, so I guess if I'm using that argument, I'm a psychopath, too. But we already knew that.

"So then why did you call?"

"I called," I say, sighing, "to make sure that you're still going to give me a ride to school tomorrow."

"Why wouldn't I be?" he asks.

"I don't know," I say. "Because there have been some weird events going on today, and so I thought if you'd decided to kick me off this trip, it would behoove you to let me know, so that I can make alternate arrangements." I just used the word "behoove" in a sentence. This is definitely not good. I'm finally cracking up.

"I'm not kicking you off the trip," he says.

"Good."

"In fact, I'd like to get back started on the trip right now," he says. "So tell me where you are and I'll come pick you up, and we'll get back on the road."

"No," I say. "I'm tired. And if you had your trip itinerary, you'd know that we're not scheduled to leave until eight o'clock. And it's only four. So we have four more hours of sleep."

"But we're not sleeping," he points out.

"Well, I would be," I say, "if you would let me off the phone." Which is obviously a lie.

"Fine," he says.

"Fine," I say.

"Wait!"

"What now?!"

"Court?"

I don't say anything.

"Are you there?"

"Yes, I'm here," I say. "What is it?"

"I love you." And then he hangs up the phone.

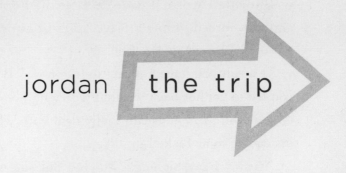

jordan the trip

Day Three, 7:56 a.m.

"Dude, I'm sorry," B. J. says. "It's all my fault."

"It isn't your fault, really," I say, sighing. "It's mine. I set up the situation, so I can't be pissed at you when I have to deal with the fallout." I'm in my hotel room, on the phone with B. J., and I just finished recounting the night's activities.

"Well, look on the bright side," he says. "At least now you don't have to worry about her finding out. She already knows."

"Yeah, that makes me feel much better," I say sarcastically, looking around the room to make sure I haven't forgotten anything. Courtney and I are supposed to get back on the road soon. Although she hasn't called me since this morning's four a.m. phone call, so who knows.

"I just mean," B. J. persists, "that maybe now you can make things right."

"What do you mean?" I ask, sitting down on the bed. To

make matters worse, I have developed a horrible headache, and was forced to buy a travel pack of aspirin at the front desk, which cost me five bucks.

"I mean you have nothing to lose now," B. J. says. "You can try to get her back without worrying about her dad and all that shit. You guys can really deal with what's going on, instead of some fucked-up fake shit."

"Yeah," I say, sighing. "Maybe. But she was pretty ripshit last night." My call waiting beeps. "That's her," I say.

"Good luck," B. J. says. I click over.

"Are you going to tell me where you are now?" I ask. I open the packet of aspirin and step into the bathroom to fill a glass of water. I feel hung over, even though I'm not.

"Are you leaving to come and get me immediately?" she asks, all bossy like.

"Yes, Courtney, I'm leaving immediately," I tell her, sighing. It's hard to balance a glass of water, the aspirin, and my phone in this tiny hotel bathroom. "Now can you tell me where you are?"

"Let me hear you actually leaving," she demands. "I'm not telling you where I am until you actually leave."

"How the hell are you supposed to know that I'm actually leaving?" I ask. I drop one of the aspirin into the sink. "Shit," I swear, grabbing it before it makes it down the drain.

"What's going on?" Courtney asks.

"Nothing," I say. "Now will you tell me where you are?" I look at the aspirin and wonder how many germs are on it and if I'll die just from putting it in my mouth. I wonder what's worse—having a headache or eating this bad aspirin.

"I want to hear you leaving," she says.

"Again, how can you hear me leaving?" I definitely need this aspirin if she's going to be acting like this all day.

"I want to hear the door close behind you."

I slam the bathroom door shut. "There," I say. "Now tell me."

"How do I know that wasn't just the bathroom door?" she asks suspiciously.

"You don't," I say. "But you were the one who came up with the criteria of how to know I was actually leaving, so don't get mad if your method isn't foolproof." I turn on the water and rinse my aspirin off, figuring an aspirin that's been rinsed off is better than an aspirin that hasn't. Besides, if it weren't for Courtney, I probably wouldn't even have thought twice about the germs. She has this uncanny need for germ-free environments and I think it's rubbed off on me.

"I can hear you running water!" Courtney says. "Unbelievable! Although I can't say I'm surprised, since you have proved yourself to be totally untrustworthy."

"Hey, do you know anything about germs in sinks?" I look at the aspirin questioningly. I really, really want that aspirin.

"What do you mean?" she asks.

"I dropped some aspirin in the sink and I want to know if it's okay to take it."

"Why can't you just throw it out and take another?" she asks, exasperated.

"Because I bought one of those travel packs that only has two pills in it," I say, still looking at the offending aspirin. Whatever. I pop it in my mouth with a copious amount of water.

"Just buy another travel pack," she says. "I wouldn't take it. It probably has sperm on it."

"Why would it have SPERM on it?" I ask, horrified. I open my mouth and look in the mirror, but it's too late. I've already swallowed it.

"Because I saw an exposé once on *20/20* about hotel rooms, and they're all covered in sperm," she says.

"Fine," I lie. "I'll buy another travel pack. Now I really am leaving, so tell me where you are."

"I'm at the Bellevue Motel," she says. "It's—"

"I know where it is," I say, sighing. We were at the same fucking motel. This whole time, we were in the same building. "I'll meet you outside in two minutes." I slide my cell phone shut and look at myself in the mirror, wondering what's more likely—me, dying from hotel bathroom germs, or Courtney ever forgiving me.

courtney | the trip →

Day Three, 11:13 a.m.

I can't believe he swallowed that disgusting pill. (Like it wasn't totally obvious.) I can't believe he was in the same hotel as me. I can't believe he told me he loved me. I can't believe I'm still on this trip.

We're in Jordan's car, on the road, and we haven't spoken for three hours. The vibe in the car isn't exactly bad. It's almost a relief, like a bunch of tension has been released, and now we can just drive.

"I have to go to the bathroom," I announce.

"Okay," Jordan says. Half an hour later, we pull into a rest stop. I'm beginning to hate rest stops. I feel like I spend half my life in a rest stop. Or in a rest stop bathroom.

I use the bathroom quickly, and try not to think about how gross it is that I've been using public bathrooms way too much lately. Although if Jordan took that aspirin, he should definitely be more concerned about his germiness

255

than I should. And good luck getting anyone to kiss him at college. I'm going to tell everyone he took a random, germ-infested sperm pill. Disgusting.

I wash my hands and dry them with a roll of suspect-looking paper towels, figuring drying my hands with gross paper towels is better than not drying them at all.

My phone rings. Jocelyn.

"Hey," I say, balancing the phone against my shoulder and tossing the paper towel into the overflowing garbage can.

"Courtney, B. J. just told me what happened," she says. "I am so, so sorry. Are you okay?"

"I'm okay," I say, sighing. I look at myself in the mirror over the sink. My eyes are a little bloodshot and my hair's a little messy, but other than that, I don't look like someone whose world is falling apart.

"Do you want to talk about it?"

"I'm sure I will, at some point," I say. "But right now, I just want to get off this trip and away from Jordan. I'm so mad, Joce."

"Yeah," she says. "I understand, but it's . . ." she trails off.

"But it's what?" I ask. "Don't even tell me you're taking his side." What a traitor.

"No, I'm not taking his side," she says. "I'm just saying, you have to remember that things aren't always completely black and white, Court."

"Yeah, well, it's black and white that he lied to me." I

feel myself starting to get mad again. I pull a brush out of my purse and start fixing my hair. Now that I'm single again, I need to look hot. So that hot, honest college guys will want me.

"Did you know he's the one that insisted you guys still go on the trip?" Jocelyn asks.

I stop brushing. "He did?"

"Yeah," Jocelyn says. "Your dad didn't want you to. But Jordan convinced him."

"How do you know that?" I ask softly.

"B. J. told me."

"But why would Jordan do that?"

"Because he wanted to spend time with you." I don't say anything. "Listen," she says. "I'm not saying what he did was right, Court. I'm just saying don't turn your back on things just because you're hurting. Try to at least think about his side of it." She hangs up, and I slide my phone back into my purse.

When I walk out of the bathroom, I almost bump into Jordan, who's standing against the soda machine.

"Watch it," I say, rolling my eyes. "I almost bumped into you."

"Courtney," he says, taking my hand. I pull away. "I want to talk about this."

"We're not talking about anything," I say, walking toward the exit. "We've talked about it enough."

"We haven't talked about it at all," he says, following me.

"And that's enough," I say. And it is. I don't want to talk about it. I don't want to deal with it. My phone starts ringing again, and I check the caller ID. It's my dad.

"Ignore it," Jordan says. We're in the parking lot now, standing near his car. I look at him. "Ignore it," he says again.

"I'm supposed to ignore *him*, but you expect me to talk to *you*?" I say, crossing my arms. That makes no sense. One of them is just as bad as the other.

"Yes," he says.

"Why?" I ask.

"Because he's your dad, and he's always going to be in your life, so it can wait," he says. "But if you and I don't deal with this now, we might end up getting into a situation that can't be repaired."

"It already can't be repaired," I say, feeling myself starting to tear up. This is why I didn't want to talk about it. Because I don't want to have to deal with this right now. I don't want to cry. I don't want to get upset. I'm enjoying the very numb, very comfortable, very avoidant feeling that I'm having right now.

"It can," he says. "Courtney, I love you."

"Don't say things like that," I say, turning around and trying to open the door to his truck. But it's locked. "It's not fair."

"What isn't?" he asks, studying me. "What's not fair? Telling you how I feel?"

"Open the door for me," I say, determined not to break down.

"No," he says. "I want to talk about this."

I don't say anything, because I know if I do, I'm going to start crying. And I don't want to give him the satisfaction of seeing me cry. We stand there for a minute, me in front of the passenger door of his truck, my back to him, him standing behind me, holding the keys. Finally, he opens the door.

"Thank you," I say, launching myself into the car. Only twelve more hours and then this trip will be over. I lay my head against the back of the seat and pray I can fall asleep.

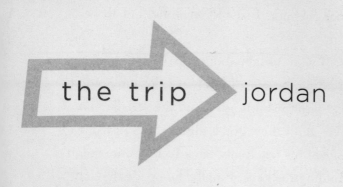

the trip > jordan

Day Three, 7:45 p.m.

Courtney doesn't say one word to me for the rest of the trip. We drive almost straight through to Boston, only stopping to go to the bathroom and grab snacks at a gas station. For the last six hours or so, she sleeps, probably because she didn't last night. Neither did I, but crazily enough, I don't feel tired.

"Court," I say when we finally pull into the front parking lot of school. "We're here."

"Mmmm," she says, opening her eyes slowly. I'm half hoping she doesn't wake up so that I'll have an excuse to touch her, to gently shake her awake, but she rubs her eyes and sits up.

There's a throng of people milling around, parents, students, all trying to find their dorm rooms. Jesus Christ. It looks like fucking Grand Central Station. I figured getting here so late would spare us most of the craziness, but apparently not.

"How was your nap?" I ask. She looks cute, her hair rumpled from sleep, her cheek red from where it was pressed against the seat.

"Can you help me with my stuff?" Courtney asks, ignoring my question. She reaches into the backseat, grabs her sweatshirt, and pulls it on.

"Yes," I say. "Court, listen, I don't—"

"Jordan," she says, holding her hand up. "I can't deal with this right now."

"But if we don't—"

She opens the car door and jumps down into the parking lot. After a second, I pop open the back of my truck, and then follow her around to the back of the car.

A perky blond girl holding a clipboard and wearing a maroon polo shirt emerges from the crowd before we have a chance to start unloading any of the stuff. "Hello!" she says. "I'm Jessica, part of your welcome orientation committee. Do you need help finding your dorm?"

"No, thanks," Courtney says. "I know where my dorm is. I mapped it all out during my tour in the fall."

Jessica's face falls, but she recovers quickly. She turns to me. "What about you?" She gives me a dazzling smile.

"No, thanks," I say. "I'm cool." I open the back of my truck, sending Jessica the silent message to go away. I want to be able to talk to Courtney before we go our separate ways, and Jessica's screwing up the plan.

"Well," she says, acting like we've made some sort of

huge mistake by not taking her help. "Here are your welcome packets, map, etc." She hands us each a huge stack of papers. Courtney and I take them obediently, even though I know I'm going to lose half this shit by tomorrow. "Do you have any questions?"

"No," Courtney says. She starts tapping her foot.

"No," I say.

"Then let me explain a little bit to you about how our meal plan works. You won't have to worry about it tonight of course, because —"

"Listen," Court starts. "We said we didn't want to hear any of this." She takes a step toward Jessica. Whoa. She must be really pissed off if she's cutting off the orientation committee chick. Wasn't her whole thing about getting oriented?

"Um, Jessica, listen," I say, deciding to step in before anything can get out of hand. I can't have Courtney fighting some girl in the parking lot, no matter how hot that would be. "We've had a really long drive, we're both tired and cranky"—Courtney raises her eyebrows—"and we just want to get to our rooms. So, thanks, really, for all your help, but we'll come and find you if we need anything."

"Okay," Jessica says, still sounding uncertain. She opens her mouth like she's about to say something else, glances at Courtney, and then changes her mind. She turns around and disappears back into the crowd.

Courtney reaches up and pulls a blue suitcase out of the truck and sets it down on the pavement.

"'Thank you, Jordan, for saving me from the scary orientation girl,'" I recite.

She ignores me and continues to unload her stuff. Okay, so apparently, trying to lighten the mood isn't the way to go. Check.

I decide to try and make normal conversation. "You have a lot of stuff," I try. "Seriously." I set a huge box down in the parking lot. "What do you have in here?"

"My books," she says. She reaches up and gathers her hair into a ponytail, then slides a hair tie around it with her other hand.

"Why would you bring books to college?" I ask her. "You know they give you books, right?" I mean it as a joke, but she gives me one of those looks, one of those "You'll never understand me" looks, so I decide it might be better to keep my mouth shut until we're done unloading everything. We spend the next half hour making trips back and forth to her dorm room. I was kind of hoping she'd want to start setting stuff up, maybe let me hang around for a while, but she just deposits stuff in a pile on her floor, presumably to deal with later. By herself.

I realize that once we're done unloading the stuff, I'm going to have to leave. So I take my time, but there's only so much and finally, all of it is in Courtney's room.

"Thanks," she says. She's standing in the doorway of her room, and I'm in the hall, and she starts to shut the door.

"Court, are we going to talk about this?" I ask, putting

my hand on the door so that she can't shut it. Well, she can shut it. Just not without breaking my hand. Hmm. On second thought, I drop my hand.

"No," she says. "We're not."

"I understand you're mad," I say. "But I want to talk about it, make you understand."

"I already understand," she says simply. She shrugs.

"You're upset now," I say, starting to become frantic. "I know that. But you need to just take a breather, I think. Take a break from me and from the trip. You're tired." I realize once I leave this room, I won't have anything to look forward to. No trip with Courtney. No seeing her every day in math. It's over. We're at college now. "Let's have breakfast tomorrow. Before orientation. I know you don't want to miss it." I smile at her then, to let her know it's okay, that I'm making a joke.

"Jordan," she says. "Please leave."

And then she shuts the door.

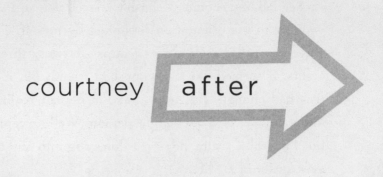

courtney after

One Day After the Trip, 9:03 a.m.

The first full day of college is overcast and gray, which is not a good omen. Bad starts and all that. I'm a big believer in the fact that the weather of the day can totally dictate how the day is going to go. So far (at least for today), this theory has been proven true.

First, I had eighteen new messages waiting for me on my voice mail when I woke up this morning. Jocelyn ("I'm worried about you, call me when you're ready."), my mom ("Courtney, honey, I want you to call me when you get this."), my dad ("Call me, we need to talk about this."), Lloyd ("It was kind of weird the way you left like that, Courtney, and I'm mad and worried."), and finally, Jordan ("Courtney, please call me, I love you."). I deleted all of them, then realized that was a horrible plan, as all it did was clear out my voice mail and leave me available to receive new messages.

Second, my roommate hasn't arrived yet, so I was stuck walking to the orientation breakfast by myself. The whole way over, all I saw were groups of twos, threes, fives, eights. It seemed like everyone had friends but me. Which was bad enough. But now that I'm here, I realize I don't know *anyone*. Not one single person. Well, except Jordan, but I'm really, really, hoping I don't run into him today. Or ever again. In my life.

I grab a plate off the pile at the end of the buffet table and load it high with eggs, pancakes, and fruit. I figure if I'm not going to be talking to anyone, then I'm going to have to keep myself busy by eating. A lot. I wish I'd brought my book. But then wouldn't I look like the loser who has to bring a book to the first day of college? If I'd known that navigating the social landscape of college was going to be so crazy, I never would have been in such a hurry to get here.

I grab an orange juice off the table of beverages, and very carefully make my way to the end of an empty table.

But once I set my stuff down, I'm stopped by a boy wearing a black T-shirt and a pair of jeans.

"Uh-oh," he says, shaking his head. He looks visibly upset, like someone's just told him his dog is sick, or that he failed a test.

"What's wrong?" I ask.

"It's just that . . ." He sighs. "You're sitting at the table where the orientation committee is supposed to sit."

"Oh," I say. "I'm sorry." I grab my plate and start to stand up. Leave it to me to sit in the one spot I'm not supposed to. I turn around and scan the dining room, but the tables have filled up fast, and there's not another empty one. Which means I'm going to have to sit with someone else. A stranger. I try to decide between a table full of girls who look like they walked off the cover of a magazine, or two girls sitting by themselves with about twenty piercings between the two of them. The pierced girls would probably be nicer, although the magazine girls look like they could have an in on the cool things to do around here. Although, God could be trying to play a trick on me for judging people on their appearances, and it could be the other way around.

"I'm afraid it's not that easy," the orientation guy says. He sighs again and runs his fingers through his short blond hair.

"What isn't?" I ask. A girl wearing a blue sequined tank top sits down with the magazine girls, nailing the last seat. Crap.

"It's just that if you sit at a table you're not supposed to during orientation, that's a disciplinary infraction." He starts flipping through the papers on his clipboard.

"What do you mean, a disciplinary infraction?" I ask, swallowing hard. This is just great. My first day of school—actually not even official school, just orientation— and I'm already in trouble. I wonder how many disciplinary infractions you can get before you get kicked out.

And if it's going to go on my permanent record. I thought at college you were supposed to have more freedom. Apparently not, if you can get in trouble just for sitting at the wrong table.

"What's your name?" the guy asks.

"Courtney," I say. "Courtney McSweeney."

"I'm Ben," he says. He holds out his hand. "Nice to meet you." He winks.

"Hold on," I say, my eyes narrowing. "Am I really in trouble?"

"No," he says, laughing. "You're not in trouble."

"So you were just messing with me?"

"Yes," he says. "But only because I wanted to know your name." He smiles, and now that I'm not worried about disciplinary infractions, I realize for the first time how cute he is. Tall, blond hair, green eyes, and a really nice smile.

"Okay," I say. "So now you know my name."

"I do," he says, nodding. "And you know mine." He leans in closer to me. "Now, I'm not really supposed to do this, but, do you want to have breakfast with me? Usually we don't let the freshmen sit at the orientation table, but I've taken up all this time talking to you, and now there're hardly any seats left." He gestures toward the crowded dining area.

"Sure," I say. "I'll sit with you." He pulls out a chair for me, but I hesitate. "Hey, Ben?" I ask.

"Yeah?"

"Do you listen to rap music?"

"Rap music?" he asks, looking confused. "No. Alternative rock. How come?"

"No reason," I say. I sit down in the chair he's offered and Ben sits down next to me.

after jordan

One Day After the Trip, 9:23 a.m.

Courtney is sitting with a guy. Some dude who's on the orientation committee. How skeezy is that? Hitting on freshmen when you're on the orientation committee. It's like hitting on students when you're a teacher. Definitely not cool.

"Hey," I say, turning to my roommate, a guy from Queens named Ricardo. Ricardo's a cool dude, one of those guys who you can tell is always going to know what's going on. Which means at some point this semester, we'll probably get in some trouble, but, hey, that's the price you pay. "What's the deal with tonight?"

"It's gonna be sick," Ricardo says. He takes a piece of toast and dips it into his over-easy eggs. There weren't over-easy eggs on the buffet, but Ricardo conned one of the dining room workers into making him one. "There're no upperclassmen on campus yet except for the orientation committee, which means it's going to be all freshmen." He smiles at me and gives me a knowing look. I pretend like I know what he means, even though I really have no idea. Does Ricardo have some knowledge of statistics pertaining to freshmen girls giving it up?

I glance over at Courtney, where she now appears to be writing her phone number down on the back of a napkin for the guy.

"Define 'sick,'" I say.

"Tons of chicks, tons of booze," he says. "It's like the official kickoff to partying in college. And the girls here," he adds, looking around the dining room, "are unfuckingbelievable."

He's right, too. The girls here are amazing. Much hotter than the ones in high school. And there's a lot more of them to choose from.

I step away from the table for a second, pull out my cell, and dial Courtney's number.

"Hey," I say into the phone. "I just wanted to tell you that I'm done. I don't want anything to do with you, so you don't have to worry about it. I'm not going to call you anymore." I snap my phone shut with a satisfied click and start thinking about what I'm going to wear to the party.

"So these girls are going to head over there with us," Ricardo says later that night. He's standing in front of the mirror, gelling his hair. From what I can tell, Ricardo spends a lot of time in front of the mirror. "You, my friend," he says to his own reflection, "are spades."

"What girls?" I ask. I'm riffling through my suitcase, try-ing to find a clean shirt to wear to the party. One of the problems with packing my shit so late was that I didn't have time to worry about if my clothes were clean or not. Therefore, I have a lot of dirty clothes in my suitcase, which is why I haven't bothered to put them in my dresser or hang them up. Why fold them when I'm just going to have to wash them anyway?

"These chicks I met at one of the orientation icebreak-ers," he says. The whole freshman class spent the afternoon playing lame icebreaker games, like "three truths and a lie" in an effort for everyone to get to know each other.

"Hot?" I pull a black button-up out of my suitcase and give it the smell test. Definitely not. I throw it back in.

"Smokin'," he says. "They're roommates, friends from high school. It's always good when the girls are friends." Ricardo picks up a bottle of cologne from his dresser and gives himself a spray.

"Jesus, that shit's strong," I say, backing away.

"It's Diddy's new cologne," he says. "It's a total pussy magnet."

"Oh."

"Anyway," he says, giving himself another spray. "I fig-ure we can head over with Chelsea and Krista, lay the groundwork. And then if it doesn't work out, we can ditch them when we get there."

This guy's good. I hold a long-sleeved blue shirt up to

my nose. Not the best, but it'll do. I pull it over my head, slide my feet into my Timberlands, and sit down on the bed.

"What time's this thing start?" It's already eleven.

"Usually things don't get going until around eleven," Ricardo says. He's making weird faces at himself in the mirror, pushing his lips out like a fish.

"What are you doing?" I ask him.

"Getting ready."

"What's that thing with your lips?"

"I read about it in some magazine. It supposedly gets your pheromones racing, so chicks want you."

"Cool." My roommate is an insane person. I don't have too much time to think about this, though, because there's a knock on the door.

"The girls," Ricardo says, opening the door. "Come in, come in." He ushers them into the room. For an insane person, Ricardo definitely knows his women. They're both blonde with big boobs. One's wearing the shortest skirt I've ever seen, and the other one is wearing a top that exposes her midriff. I realize I haven't hooked up with anyone since I've been with Courtney. And now that Courtney and I are broken up, I can hook up with one of these girls. Maybe both of them. I feel myself starting to get turned on.

"I'm Jordan," I say.

"Chelsea," one says.

"Krista," the other one says. I'm never going to be able to tell them apart.

We head over to the party, and Ricardo makes it easy for me by latching on to the taller one (Krista, I think), and so I drop back and start talking to Chelsea. I'm starting to think that for all of Ricardo's weirdness, he and I might get along just fine. Unlike B. J., he has play. Ricardo obviously knows the first rule of the double hookup, which is that when two guys are out with two girls, you immediately pair off in an effort to let the girls know a hookup is definitely expected.

Chelsea and I do the required small talk on the way to the party. I find out she's from Boston, an elementary education major, and really, really likes to party. I know this because she says, "Do you like to party?" and I say, "Yeah, I guess," and she says, "Well, I really, really like to party."

By the time we get to the frat house, the festivities are in full swing. There are people all over the place—outside, inside, on the porch, on the lawn. It seems like the whole freshman class is here.

I grab two cups of beer from the keg and take them over to where Chelsea's waiting for me by the door.

"Here," I say.

"Thanks." She takes a few huge gulps. Whoa. This girl doesn't fuck around.

"So what dorm are you in?" I ask.

"I live off campus," she tells me, and then smiles. The strap of her bra is showing. Red. Hot.

"No shit," I say. "How'd you manage that?"

"My parents pay for everything," she says. "They feel

guilty that they're never around, so they make up for it by trying to give me everything I want."

"That sounds sweet," I say, wondering if she'll give me pointers on how I can finagle that situation for myself. My parents already give me pretty much whatever I want, but making my mom feel guilty is very appealing.

We talk for a little longer, and drink even more, and half an hour later, I've got quite the buzz going on. I can't stop looking at her bra strap. This girl is seriously hot. I wonder if it's because she's a college girl. But that really makes no sense, since until a few months ago, she wasn't in college, and it's unlikely that she's morphed into a hottie in just a few months.

"Hey," she says, leaning into me. "We can probably get out of here now, if you want."

Her lips are a few inches from mine, and I can feel my body responding to hers. She smells like beer and perfume and something sexy. "Yeah," I say, leaning back into her. "What did you have in mind?"

"We could go back to my place," she says.

"Go back to your place?" I ask.

"Yeah," she says. "And watch movies. I have a flatscreen and tons of DVDs." For some reason, Courtney's face flickers across my brain, but I push it away. Fuck Courtney, I think. This chick is hot. The thing with Courtney is over. I take another sip of my drink, figuring if I can just get a little more buzzed, I'll be fine.

"That sounds cool," I say. "Just let me tell Ricardo."

I start making my way through the crowd, and finally find Ricardo standing by the keg with his arm around a brunette. I'm impressed. Anyone who comes to a party and then hooks up with a different girl than the one he brought, has to have serious game.

"I'm leaving," I say. "I'm going back to Chelsea's apartment."

"Sweet," he says. "Nice one, bro. I'll catch you later."

But when I turn back around, I see Courtney in the corner, talking to that guy she was with at orientation. She's leaning against the wall, and he leans in to whisper something in her ear. She throws her head back and laughs, her hair falling down around her face. My stomach feels like it's in my throat, and then someone walks in front of me, blocking my view.

"Hey," Chelsea says, grabbing my arm. "There you are. I was wondering what was taking you so long." She leans into me again. "Are you ready to go?" I can feel her breath against my ear, and her chest against my shoulder.

"I'm sorry," I say to Chelsea. "I . . . I can't go with you."

And then I walk out of the party, down the street, and back to my dorm.

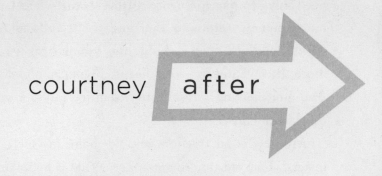

courtney after

Two Days After the Trip, 1:53 a.m.

I get home from my first college party to find a voice mail from Jordan on my cell. He left it earlier this morning, but I left my cell phone in my room all day, in an effort to not have to deal with anyone. "I'm done," the message says. "I don't want anything to do with you, so you don't have to worry about it."

Good, I think. I don't have to worry about you. In fact, I was just at a party with Ben, the guy I met at orientation. The *sophomore* I met at orientation. The older guy who doesn't listen to rap music, and who went out for pizza with me afterwards.

Although, his friends were kind of obnoxious. One spilled beer on his hand and then wiped it on my sweater. And I think Ben might have laughed. But I'm sure it was about something else. And then, at the pizza place, I had to pay. But whatever. I'm not materialistic or anything. I don't need guys to pay for me. And besides, it wasn't even that much money. Although Ben and his friends all got extra cheese without even asking me, which was two dollars more. But whatever. The point is, I went to a college party. And I'm meeting guys. Better, mature guys. I don't need Jordan anymore.

My newfound freedom should make me feel good, but instead, I am starting to get angry. What is he talking about, he's done? *I'm* the one who's done with *him*. I'm the one who decided never to talk to him again. Not the other way around.

The door to my room opens and a girl with shoulder-length brown hair walks in. She's wearing a cute jean skirt and a navy blue zip-up hoodie. "Hey!" she says. "You must be Courtney. I'm Emma." She holds her hand out, and I take it. "I got here late," she says. "My flight was delayed."

"Oh," I say, looking around the room. I was so caught up in Jordan's ridiculous voice mail that I didn't even notice there's someone else's stuff in the room. There are clothes in the other closet, a computer on the other desk, and the other bed is made up.

"I'm sorry, was it okay to leave all my stuff?" Emma asks, looking worried. "I didn't have a chance to completely unpack because I didn't want to miss orientation, and I tried to move it out of the way, but—"

"Oh, no, it's fine," I say. "It wasn't in the way."

"Oh, okay," she says, looking confused.

"I'm sorry," I say, realizing I'm not being the most friendly roommate. "My psycho ex-boyfriend just left me a message, which really pissed me off."

"Really?" she says, looking interested. She plops down on her bed, and lays upside down, with her feet on the pillow. "What's the deal?"

"He did something really mean to me," I say. "And I told him to screw off." Emma nods. "And then . . . Then he leaves me a message saying 'I won't be contacting you again.'"

"Okay . . ." Emma looks confused. My roommate thinks I'm crazy.

"Like it was his idea that we don't talk anymore! That's ridiculous! That's insane! That's . . ." I feel myself starting to get madder and madder. "Do you have your student directory?" I ask her.

She reaches over and pulls it out of her night table. "Thanks." I open it to the Rs and slide my finger down the list until I get to Jordan's name. Good, he's not that far from here. "I'll be back in a few minutes," I say.

"Okay," Emma says again, still sounding uncertain.

I march down the hallway and out into the night. I don't care that it's two in the morning. I don't care that his roommate might be sleeping. It's about time someone let Jordan know he can't just treat girls like this, constantly using them for his own agenda. I need to stand up for myself.

When I get to his dorm room, I can hear music coming

from inside. Rap. Of course. I knock on the door. Loudly. I hope he gets a noise complaint, and his RA throws him out of school.

"Jordan!" I say. "I need to talk to you."

I hear a rustling sound in the room, and for a second, I lose a little steam. What if he has a girl over? What if he left me that message to make himself feel better, to make it known to me that it was over, so that he wouldn't have to feel bad if he thought he was cheating on me? What if he thinks I'm the psycho one? I guess showing up at his room at two in the morning isn't the best way to combat that, but whatever.

I knock on the door louder. "I know you're in there!" I'm practically screaming.

He opens the door. "Hey," he says.

"Are you alone?"

"Yeah, why?"

"I don't know," I say. I cross my arms. "First night of college and all. Figured you'd want to christen the room."

"Yeah, well, I figured I'd take the night off, *slowly* settle into college. Unlike you." He looks pissed.

"What's that supposed to mean?"

A door opens across the hall, and a guy in a pair of gray boxers pokes his head out into the hall. "Hey," he says. "Could you keep it down? I'm trying to sleep."

"Sorry," Jordan says. He motions to me as if to say "Psycho girls, what can you do about them?"

"Don't even," I say. "This is your fault, and you know it."

"What's my fault?" he asks. "And if you're going to be yelling at me, would you like to come in? I don't think my neighbors want to listen to this."

"No," I say, throwing up my hands in exasperation. "I do not want to come in."

"Then why did you come over here?" he asks, crossing his arms. He's wearing a white T-shirt and a pair of red-and-black mesh shorts. He looks like he was laying around in bed. Must. Not. Let. Hotness. Distract. Me.

"I came over here," I say, "because of that ridiculous message you left on my voice mail."

"What was so ridiculous about it?" he asks. "That's what you wanted, right? For me to leave you alone."

"Yes," I say. "I did."

"Did? Or do?"

"Do!" I say. "I don't want anything to do with you."

"Then why did you come over here?"

"Because!" I say, throwing my hands up at his obvious stupidity. "Because I want to make sure you know that it's my decision."

"What is?" He frowns.

"The decision to not talk anymore. It my decision." I cross my arms and tap my foot.

"Sure," he says. "Whatever you say."

"It is."

"Fine."

"Fine!"

I turn on my heel and start walking down the hall, but he yells after me, "Be careful about Upperclass Joe, there."

"Who?"

"The guy you've been all over all day."

I swallow. How does he know about that? "How do you know about that?" I ask. "And I haven't been all over him all day."

"Well, whatever," he says. "Just be careful."

The door across the hall opens again, and the same guy pops his head out. "Seriously," he says, sounding really annoyed.

"Sorry, dude, " Jordan repeats, not really sounding it. He looks at me. "Look, do you want to come in? Because for someone who's not talking to me, you certainly seem to have a lot to say."

"You do," the guy across the hall agrees. "And you should go in and talk about it. Otherwise I'm not going to get any sleep."

"Fine," I say. I push past Jordan and into his room. He shuts the door behind me. His room is a little smaller than mine, and he still hasn't unpacked his stuff. His comforter is thrown over his bed, and it looks like he was laying on top of it. Probably because he didn't pack extra-long sheets.

He sits down on the bed. "Do you want to sit down?" he asks, motioning to his desk chair.

"No," I say. I stand in the middle of the room. Neither of us say anything.

Finally, he sighs. "You can't keep running away from things, Court."

"I'm not," I say. "Just because I don't want to deal with you, doesn't mean I'm running away from things."

"Oh, really?" he says. "Have you talked to your dad?"

"No."

"Lloyd?"

"No."

He raises his eyebrows at me.

"That doesn't mean I'm running away from things," I say. "It just means that I don't want to talk to anyone right now."

"You're talking to me," he says. I don't say anything. "Courtney, I need to know if there's a chance. If you can forgive me, if there's . . ." he trails off, and I look at him. He's looking at me with this genuine expression on his face, and I can hear in his voice that he really means it. Just like the first night he called me and wanted to hang out and it made no sense to me, but I could still hear in his voice that he really wanted to.

"I can't," I say, shaking my head. "You lied to me, Jordan. If you loved me, you wouldn't have done that."

"It's not always that black and white, Courtney," he says, running his fingers through his hair. "It's not."

"It is to me," I say. My heart's beating fast now, and I can feel the adrenaline racing through my body. "I would never have done what you did to me."

"Maybe not," he says. "And I'm not trying to say that what I did was right. But I freaked out. I'm in love with you. I thought you were going to hate me. I thought you were going to blame me for not telling you. I had just found out my mom was cheating on my dad. It was fucked up, Court."

He looks at me then, and I feel something soften inside me.

"You didn't handle it the right way," I say, and I can tell I'm going to start crying.

"I know that now," he says. He takes a step closer to me, and this time, I don't pull back. "And I wish I would have handled it differently. I wish I could have seen through all the insanity and just talked to you. But I don't want to make that mistake again. I want to talk about this." He's close to me now, and he reaches out and puts his arms around me.

"I'm really upset right now, Jordan," I tell him, being honest for the first time. "You really upset me. With everything. Breaking up with me, keeping things from me."

"I know," he says. "And I'm sorry. I didn't do it on purpose, Court. I couldn't stand the thought of you hating me, so I just chose not to deal with it. But I'm not going to do it anymore. I'm going to deal with it. *We* have to deal with it."

"How?" I ask, and his arms are around me now, and I'm crying and my eyes are making wet spots on his shirt but he's not pulling away.

"By doing whatever it takes," he says simply.

"Do you know . . . I mean, do you know what they're going to do? About things? My dad and your mom?" I pull away for a second and look at him, knowing that whatever the answer is, it won't be good.

"I'm not sure," he says. He hesitates. "My mom told my brother she was leaving my dad, but I'm not sure if she's really thought it through, or if she'll really do it."

I nod.

"We'll get through it," he says, pulling me close again.

"I don't know," I say. "I don't know if it's going to ever be the same."

"That's okay," he says. "That you don't know, I mean. But if there's even a chance, then I want to try."

I look at him then, and I see how hurt he is. I think about how awful it must have been for him to find out his mom was cheating on his dad, and even more awful that he felt he couldn't tell me. I think about how people make mistakes, and how I lied to him about the Lloyd thing, and how emotions and heartbreak and love can really screw with your head. Most of all, I think about how it is to be with him, and how if there's even a chance we can be together, I can't be afraid to find out.

He kisses me then, softly on the lips, and I lean into his body. "You're going to be okay, Court," he whispers into my ear, and I know he's talking about the stuff with my family, not with him and I.

"I know," I say. "And I wish you had known that, too.

You can't always protect me from everything. I can be strong, too, you know."

"I know that now," he says. "And isn't that what matters?" He looks at me then, and we're kissing and his hands are on my body. We fall onto his bed, and he pulls away for a second to look at me. "I love you, Court," he says.

"I love you, too."

And then he holds me until I fall asleep.

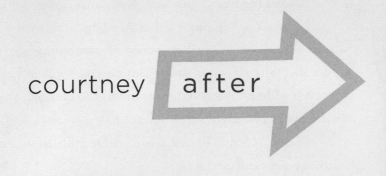

courtney after

Two Days After the Trip, 10:01 a.m.

"Hey," my roommate says the next morning when I get back to our room. She's sitting at her computer, messing around on MySpace. "I take it things either went really, really well or really, really bad."

"What do you mean?" I ask.

"Well, you never came home last night. Which means you either made up with your boyfriend, or you didn't make up with him, and spent the rest of the night trolling around the streets, looking for mischief. Or holed up with some other random guy. Or crying your eyes out in an alley."

I giggle. "It went . . . well, let's just say I'm being cautiously optimistic."

"Good," she says, smiling. "Cautiously optimistic is good."

"Hey," I say. "I'm sorry about last night. I'm not crazy, I swear. I just have a lot of stuff going on."

"Not a big deal," she says. She shuts down her computer and picks up her purse. "I'm heading over to the financial aid office, because they screwed something up with my forms." She rolls her eyes. "But do you want to have breakfast together? We could meet at around eleven? You can tell me about last night."

"Sure," I say. "I have some phone calls to make now, so that works out perfect."

"Cool." She smiles.

Once the door shuts behind her, I pick up my cell phone and take a deep breath. I have to call Lloyd. I have to call my mom, my dad, and Jocelyn. I told Jordan he had to stop protecting me, and now I have to stop protecting myself. I decide to go for it, to jump right into things, to make the hardest call first. I dial my dad's number at work. The sun is shining through the window, casting stripes of light on the floor. "Hey," I say when he answers. "It's me."

about the author

Lauren Barnholdt was born and raised in Syracuse, New York, and currently resides in central Connecticut. She is the author of *The Secret Identity of Devon Delaney*, and her first novel for teens, *Reality Chick*, was a *Teen People* "Can't-Miss Pick." When she's not writing, Lauren likes to read, blog, and reorder her Netflix queue three million times. Although she's been on numerous road trips, none of them have been with a guy who dumped her. Visit Lauren's website at www.laurenbarnholdt.com or her MySpace page at www.myspace.com/laurenbarnholdtbooks.

WANTED

Single Teen Reader in search of a FUN romantic comedy read!

How NOT to Spend Your Senior Year
CAMERON DOKEY

Royally Jacked
NIKI BURNHAM

Ripped at the Seams
NANCY KRULIK

Cupidity
CAROLINE GOODE

Spin Control
NIKI BURNHAM

South Beach Sizzle
SUZANNE WEYN &
DIANA GONZALEZ

She's Got the Beat
NANCY KRULIK

30 Guys in 30 Days
MICOL OSTOW

Animal Attraction
JAMIE PONTI

A Novel Idea
AIMEE FRIEDMAN

Scary Beautiful
NIKI BURNHAM

Getting to Third Date
KELLY McCLYMER

Dancing Queen
ERIN DOWNING

Major Crush
JENNIFER ECHOLS

Do-Over
NIKI BURNHAM

Love Undercover
JO EDWARDS

Prom Crashers
ERIN DOWNING

Gettin' Lucky
MICOL OSTOW

Available from Simon Pulse ♥♥ Published by Simon & Schuster

What's your reality?

FIND OUT WITH THESE HAUNTING NOVELS.

I HEART YOU,
YOU HAUNT ME

FAR FROM YOU

SWOON

THE HOLLOW

DEVOURED

RAVEN

KISSED BY AN ANGEL

DARK SECRETS

From Simon Pulse | Published by Simon & Schuster